SO-EIK-824

Mechanical Drives 1 Student Reference

HB502

FIRST EDITION, v5.05000
XE00AEN

Amatrol, AMNET, CIMSOFT, MCL, MINI-CIM, IST, ITC, VEST, and Technovate are trademarks or registered trademarks of Amatrol, Incorporated. All other brand and product names are trademarks or registered trademarks of their respective companies.

Copyright © 2019 by AMATROL, INC.

All rights Reserved. No part of this publication may be reproduced, translated, or transmitted in any form or by any means, electronic, optical, mechanical, or magnetic, including but not limited to photographing, photocopying, recording or any information storage and retrieval system, without written permission of the copyright owner.

AMATROL, INC.
2400 CENTENNIAL BLVD.
JEFFERSONVILLE, INDIANA 47130 USA
PHONE 812-288-8285
FAX 812-283-1584
www.amatrol.com

Table of Contents

Module 1 Introduction to Mechanical Drive Systems

Segment 1 Mechanical Power Transmission Safety

Objective 1 Describe the Function of a Mechanical Power Transmission System and Give an Advantage

Components of a Mechanical Power Transmission System

A mechanical power transmission system is a device composed of linkages, shafts, bearings, gears, pulleys, or other components whose purpose is to transmit and control the force and motion from one device to another.

The device from which the transmission system receives power is called the driver, or prime mover, and the device it transmits power to is called the driven device.

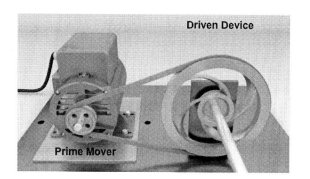

Other Types of Power Transmission Systems

In this example, a V-belt drive system transmits power from an electric motor to an air compressor.

Three other methods to transmit power besides the mechanical power transmission are electrical, thermal, and fluid.

An example of electrical power transmission is an electric motor. A gas engine is an example of thermal power transmission. Hydraulic or pneumatic actuators are examples of fluid power transmission.

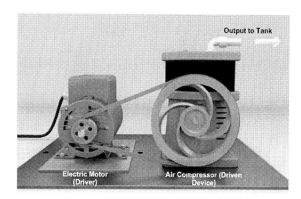

Example of Other Types of Power Transmission Systems

In most cases, the mechanical system is used in combination with one of these other forms of power.

For example, the machine shown here uses an electric motor to convert electrical power into mechanical power in the form of a rotating shaft.

The mechanical system then transmits the power to another rotating shaft to drive a compressor, which converts the mechanical power into fluid power.

Coupled Transmission Systems

Coupling the electric motor directly to the shaft of the compressor is another approach. This does not eliminate the mechanical system as you might think. It just changes it from a belt drive system to a direct coupled system.

Advantages and Disadvantages of Coupled Transmission Systems

Some reasons to use a more complex mechanical system than a direct coupling system are:

- To increase or decrease the speed
- To increase or decrease the torque or force
- To change the direction of motion
- To extend the power to a location that is remote to the driver or prime mover
- To change the type of motion from rotary to linear
- To control the acceleration and deceleration of the motion

Objective 2   Describe Five Methods of Rotary Mechanical Power Transmission and Give an Application of Each

Mechanical Power Transmission Directions

Mechanical power is transmitted in either a linear or rotary direction. Rotary power transmission in the form of a shaft-to-shaft transmission is by far the most common.

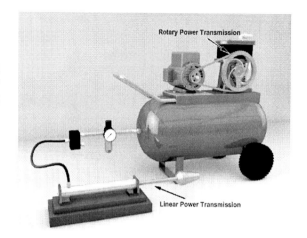

Two Categories of Rotary Power Transmission

Two categories of rotary power transmission are:

• Axial
• Shaft-to-Adjacent-Shaft

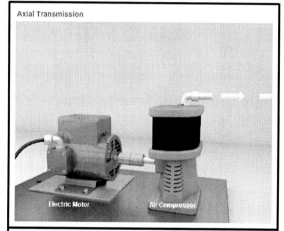

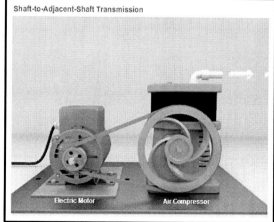

Axial Power Transmission

Two commonly used methods of axial power transmission are coupling and clutch.

The coupling connects two shafts together. The most common application of the coupling is to connect a driver to a driven component, as in an electric motor and pump.

Another application is to extend the length of a shaft by connecting it to another shaft.

Clutch Description

A clutch, like the coupling, connects two shafts together. The difference is the clutch allows the two shafts to disconnect and connect to each other while they are running.

A common application of a clutch is overrunning. An example of overrunning is a fan driven by a diesel engine.

When the diesel engine shuts down, it stops very quickly. A clutch is used to disconnect the fan so that it can coast to a stop. The clutch prevents putting strain on the engine caused by stopping the fan suddenly.

Three Types of Shaft-to-Adjacent-Shaft Power Transmission

There are three types of shaft-to-adjacent-shaft power transmission:

- Belt Drive
- Chain Drive
- Gear Drive

Belt Drive

A belt drive uses a belt made of either synthetic or natural rubber that is stretched around two rotating smooth hubs.

Belt drives are commonly found on compressors and fans.

Chain Drive

The chain drive works similarly to the belt drive, except that it uses a metal chain wrapped around two hubs that have teeth.

Chain drives are commonly found on small vehicles.

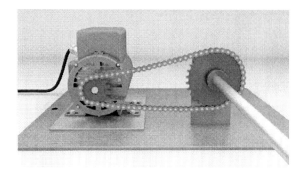

Gear Drive

The gear drive uses rotating hubs that have teeth meshed together.

Gear drives are used when the distances between shafts are very close, the direction of motion must take a right angle turn, the change in speed and torque is very high, or the drive must be sealed.

Gear drives are commonly found in gearboxes, machine tool drives, and rollers.

Similarities of Three Types of Shaft-to-Adjacent-Shaft Power Transmissions

All three types of drives are commonly used to increase or decrease the speed and torque transmitted to the drive shaft by selecting different sizes for the hubs.

Also, all three drives extend the power to a location different than that of the driver. Chain and belt drives are usually used when the distances between shafts are greater.

Objective 3   Describe Six Rules of Safe Dress for Working with Power Transmission Equipment

Workplace Safety

Workplace safety is important in every job.

Jobs that involve mechanical equipment can be very dangerous because there are moving parts that transmit high forces.

Many experienced mechanical workers have missing fingers or hands as a result of their work around mechanical systems. However, you can help avoid this by practicing dress safety rules.

Six Dress Safety Rules

The purpose of dress safety rules is to keep you or your clothing from getting caught in the moving parts of a machine.

Wear safety glasses at all times.

Avoid wearing loose-fitting clothes.

Remove ties, watches, rings, and other jewelry.

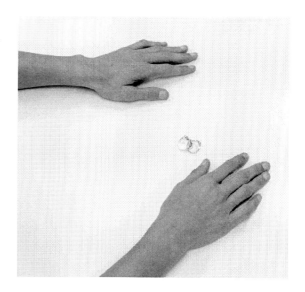

Tie up long hair or put it in a cap or under your shirt.

Wear heavy-duty leather shoes. Steel-toed shoes are recommended. Canvas shoes are not acceptable.

Roll up long sleeves or wear short sleeves.

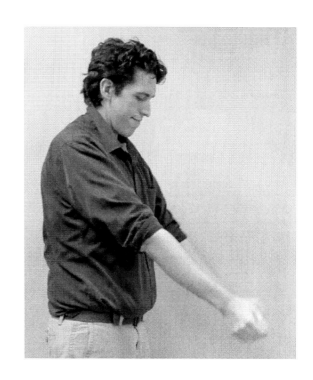

Gloves and Running Machinery

Do not wear gloves around machinery when
it is running. Gloves can get caught in the
moving components and pull your hand into
the machine.

Objective 4   Describe Eight Mechanical Transmission Safety Rules

Eight Mechanical Transmission Safety Rules

In addition to dress rules, there are other rules you should follow while working with machinery. These include:

- Make sure machine power is off and its power switch is locked out by a lockout/tagout device.
- Do not enter the machine's area of operation until the machine is completely stopped.
- Always keep your tools clean and organized.
- Do not work on wet floors.
- Make sure all guards are in place before operating the machine.
- Always get help when lifting heavy parts.
- Make sure that you announce that you are going to start a machine before doing so to give others a chance to clear the area.
- Make sure that no one is in the area before starting a machine.

Objective 5   Describe the Operation of the Lockout/Tagout System

How to Perform a Lockout/Tagout

One of the greatest dangers to a mechanic, electrician, or technician is to have another person power up equipment while they are working on it.

In order to avoid this possible danger, lock out all power sources when performing maintenance on the equipment so that it cannot be turned on accidentally.

This is accomplished by using a two-step process called lockout/tagout.

• Lockout
• Tagout

Lockout

Lockout is the process of blocking the energy flow from a power source to a piece of equipment and ensuring that it remains blocked.

A lockout device such as a lock, block, or chain at the power source prevents a piece of equipment from receiving power from the source.

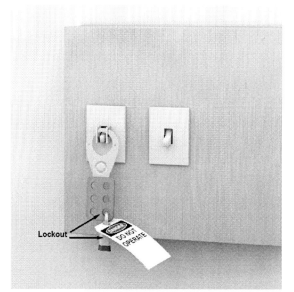

Tagout

Tagout involves placing a tag on the power source that warns others not to restore power. The tags must clearly state: Do not operate.

Tags must be applied by hand. There are special occasions to use a tagout without a lockout. However, take special care because a tagout is not a physical restraint like a lockout.

Tagout

Installing and Removing a Lockout/Tagout

Any person who is going to work around or on the piece of equipment should perform a lockout/tagout. The only person who should remove a lockout/tagout is the person who installed it.

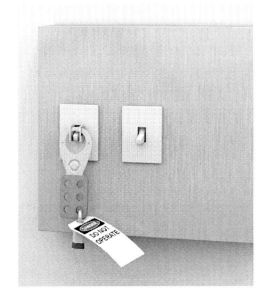

Multiple Lockouts

In a case where there are several persons servicing a piece of equipment, a multiple lockout is used so that each person has their own lockout on the equipment.

In order to restore the power, everyone must remove their own locks. This ensures that everyone is clear of the equipment before starting it.

All companies are required to develop a lockout/tagout procedure and must train the employees on the procedure.

Segment 2   Machine Installation

Objective 6   Describe the Function of a Foundation and Give Three Types

Definition and Purpose of a Foundation

A foundation is the structure that supports the machine. The foundation for a machine is important to its life and performance.

It must be designed to perform three functions:

• Support the load of the machine without settling
• Maintain the alignment between coupled components
• Absorb any vibrations created by the machine or surrounding equipment

Three Types of Foundations

The foundations of most heavy equipment consist of one of three materials:

• Solid concrete
• Reinforced concrete
• Structural steel

The solid concrete foundation is best. However, reinforced concrete or structural steel foundations are less expensive.

A typical concrete foundation is shown here. As you can see, anchor bolts are imbedded in the concrete to attach the machine to the foundation.

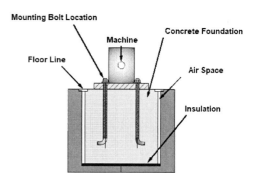

Objective 7   Describe the Function and Construction of a Bedplate

The Importance of a Bedplate

It is very important to mount the driver of the mechanical transmission in such a way that it can be aligned with the mechanical devices it is to drive and that its alignment is maintained during operation.

A machine that has independent components that must be aligned with each other should not be mounted directly to a foundation.

Instead, mount the machine to a bedplate, which is, in turn, mounted to a foundation.

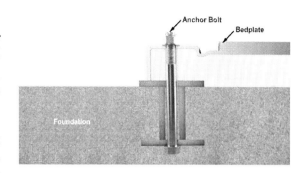

The Description of a Bedplate

The bedplate is a solid piece of metal, usually made of steel. It provides a rigid, level surface for mounting, which helps with components' alignment.

The bedplate is anchored to the foundation with anchor bolts and is filled in with grout. Grout is a type of concrete that provides support to the bedplate, giving it more rigidity.

Before anchoring the bedplate, however, it should first be leveled. Leveling means to make the surface of the bedplate parallel to the ground. The bedplate can be leveled by shimming it with double-wedge shims or with flat shims.

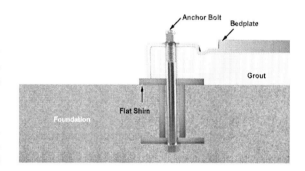

Objective 8   Describe the Function of a Spirit Level and Give an Application

An Example of a Spirit Level

The device most often used to check the level of a surface, such as a bedplate, is a spirit level, or level. A typical example is shown here.

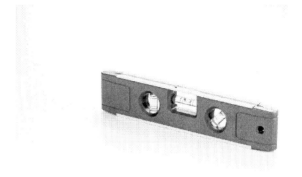

The Function of a Spirit Level

There are many applications where it is important to orient a surface so that it is either parallel or perpendicular to the ground.

This is commonly done in building construction with walls and floors, as well as in industry with machinery.

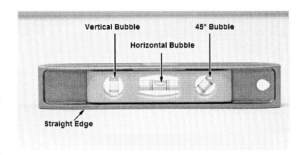

Spirit Level Measurements

The spirit level is usually designed so that you can measure the perpendicularity as well as the parallelism of a surface with the ground.

Objective 9   Describe the Operation of a Spirit Level

The Components of a Spirit Level

A spirit level consists of a bar with precision ground metal edges and liquid-filled tubes.

The precision ground edges act as straight edges to place against the surface being checked. The liquid-filled tubes are oriented both parallel and perpendicular to the straight edge surfaces.

Each tube has a bubble in it and is inscribed with two alignment marks. These bubbles and alignment marks are used to determine if the surface is parallel to the ground or perpendicular to the ground.

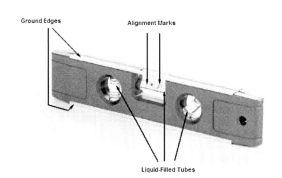

Horizontal Use of a Spirit Level

Use the spirit level to measure both vertical and horizontal surfaces.

Use the horizontal bubble to measure the parallelism of a horizontal surface to the ground.

When the bubble is positioned precisely between the two marks, the surface is parallel to the ground.

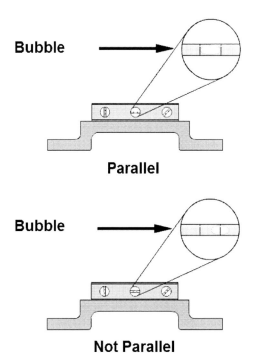

Vertical Use of a Spirit Level

In a similar manner, you can see here how to measure the perpendicularity of a vertical surface to the ground.

Use a vertical bubble to do this. When the bubble is positioned precisely between the two marks, the surface is perpendicular to the ground.

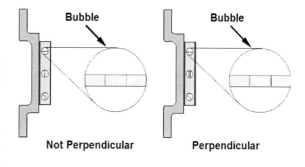

Not Perpendicular   Perpendicular

Segment 3 Motor Mounting

Objective 10 Describe Three Types of Motor Mounts and Give an Application of Each

Three Types of Motor Mounts

The motor that drives a mechanical transmission can be mounted to a bedplate in one of three ways:

- Foot Mount
- C-Face Mount
- Adjustable Mount

Foot Mount

The foot mount is a simple and common method of mounting an electric motor. A foot mount consists of tabs or feet, attached at the four corners of the motor.

Each foot has a mounting hole allowing the motor to be fastened to a bedplate with a bolt. The foot mounts of a larger motor are usually made from a steel plate and are welded to the base of the motor.

Smaller motors often have a one-piece steel plate with four holes in it.

Foot Mount

C-Face Mount

One of the problems with a foot mount is that the motor must be carefully aligned with the other components connected to it. The C-face mounting method solves this problem by mounting the driven component directly to the motor face.

This requires the motor and the driven component to have a special face called a C-face, which has a flange and bolt holes. The C-face still requires some alignment but it is a much less tedious process than with the foot mount.

The C-face mounting is commonly used with turbine pumps. It is also used with pumps that are small enough to hang from the motor and the application is compatible with direct drive.

The gearbox is another application where the C-face is used, except that the motor can often hang from the gearbox.

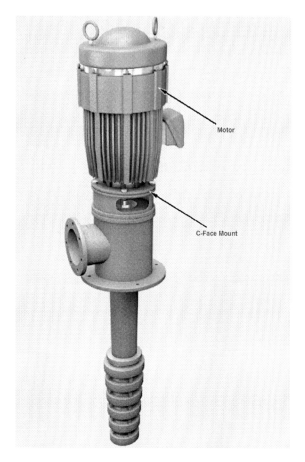

Motor

C-Face Mount

Adjustable Mount

An adjustable motor mount is a third method of motor mounting used with a foot mount. With the adjustable motor mount the motor is mounted on a bedplate.

The adjustable motor mount contains a screw that can move the motor back and forth on one axis. This allows the motor to be moved without having to loosen the mounting bolts.

The adjustable motor mount is often used when it is necessary to routinely change the position of the motor to change tension on a belt or chain drive.

All service lines such as power, air, and water must have enough flexibility to move with the machine as it adjusts.

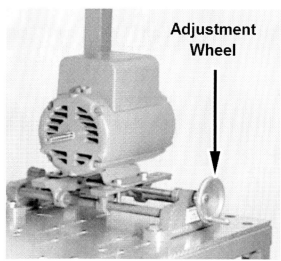

Adjustment Wheel

Objective 11 Describe How Fasteners Are Used to Attach a Motor Mount to a Bedplate

The Components of a Fastener

Mounting a motor starts with selecting a fastener to use to attach the motor to the bedplate. Most often you should use a hex head bolt with two flat washers, a lock washer, and nut.

The plain, flat washer makes sure that the bolt will not pull through the mounting hole, and the lock washer makes sure that the nut does not become loose.

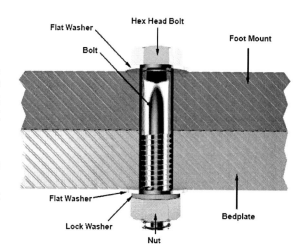

Thread Locking Adhesive Description

As an alternative to the lock washer, you can use Loctite® 242 thread-locking adhesive. It is intended for general-purpose use for one quarter inch diameter and larger screws.

The fastener can be removed with hand tools.

Objective 12   Describe How to Select Fastener Size and Type for a Motor Mount

Six Fastener Features

When selecting a fastener to use with a motor mount, take care to pick the correct fastener. There are several features to consider when selecting a fastener:

- Diameter
- Grade
- Thread Type
- Length
- Washer Thickness
- Nut Thickness/Grade

Diameter

The bolt size should be as large as possible to fit through the hole in the foot mount and still allow a little room for alignment.

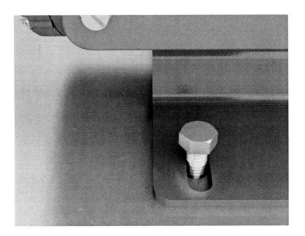

This means that you should select a bolt diameter that fills up most of the mounting hole, but not all. For example, a 7/16-inch bolt could be used for a 1/2-inch hole.

Grade

The bolt's grade should be either a grade 5 or, for heavier applications, a grade 8. This is because the higher grade of bolt has a larger value of strength.

The markings on the bolt head identify the grade of the bolt. The grade of the bolt is the number of raised lines on the head plus two.

Grade Marking on Bolt Head	SAE Number	Tensile Strength
	2	64,000 psi
	5	105,000 psi
	6	130,000 psi
	8	150,000 psi

Three raised lines indicate a grade 5. Zero raised lines indicate a grade 2.

A nut should have the same grade as the bolt. Dots identify the grade of a nut.

Thread Type

The coarse thread type (UNC) is commonly used for motor mounting applications. Assembly and disassembly of the UNC is quicker than the fine thread type (UNF) because it has fewer threads per inch.

Coarse Thread   Fine Thread

Length

The initial length of the bolt is determined by the thickness of the parts, washers, and nut. Once this has been determined, the final length is selected as the next longer standard bolt length. Common sized bolt lengths are typically available in 1/4-inch increments.

Washer Thickness

Determine the thickness of washers by measuring them or by using a catalog specification. Remember that a lock washer lies flat when locked down by the nut.

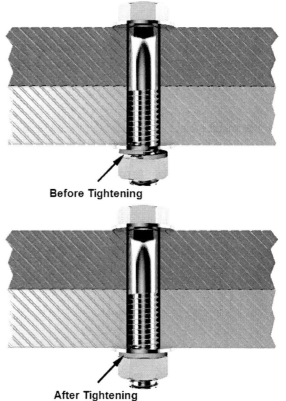

Before Tightening

After Tightening

Nut Thickness/Grade

The nut thickness varies depending on the size of the bolt. For most applications, the thickness of the nut should equal the root diameter of the bolt's threads.

Only use thicker or thinner nuts in special cases, such as when there is limited assembly space.

Nuts can be obtained in the same grades as bolts. A nut should not be used that has a lower grade than the bolt it is used with. The grade markings on nuts are typically raised dots or slashes arranged in a pattern determined by engineering standards.

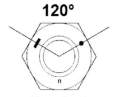

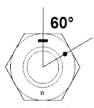

Objective 13   Describe How to Mount and Level an Electric Motor

Preparation for Motor Mounting and Leveling

First select the fasteners. Then mount and level the motor. During the mounting process, also check the motor mounting for:

• Shaft Run-Out
• Shaft End Float
• Soft Foot

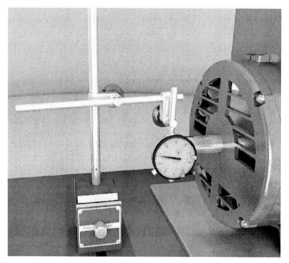

The Soft Foot Condition

Soft foot is a condition where one or more of the mounting feet are not level with the others or where the base plate is not level in all places. This causes the motor to not rest on all four feet.

An uneven mounting surface or an uneven motor mount can cause a soft foot. Small motors often have a soft foot because their foot mounts are made of thin metal and warp easily.

Soft Foot Condition Common Causes

Here are some other types and causes of a soft foot condition.

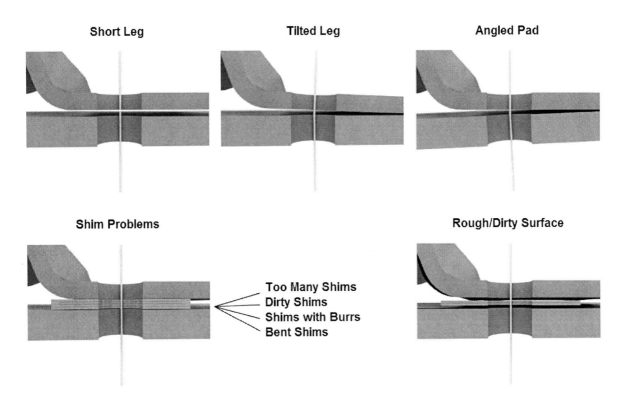

Short Leg Tilted Leg Angled Pad

Shim Problems
- Too Many Shims
- Dirty Shims
- Shims with Burrs
- Bent Shims

Rough/Dirty Surface

Problems That Occur Due to a Soft Foot

There are several mishaps that can occur due to a soft foot. Therefore, a soft foot must be corrected before placing a motor into service.

The nuts securing the feet to the base may loosen. This can result in looseness and misalignment that causes vibration that is dangerous to you and to the machinery.

Metal fatigue may occur at the soft foot and cracks can develop, or the soft foot could even break off.

Soft Foot Condition

How to Check and Correct a Soft Foot

To fix a soft foot, simply shim the one short leg, or soft foot, so that the motor rests solidly on all four feet. In general, machines should not have a soft foot greater than 0.002 inch.

Correcting Soft Foot

Check and correct a soft foot using a two-step process:

• Initial Soft Foot
• Final Soft Foot

Initial Soft Foot

Before setting the machine in place, remove all dirt, rust, and burrs from the bottom of the machine's feet, the shims to be used, and the mounting base at the areas where the machine's feet will rest.

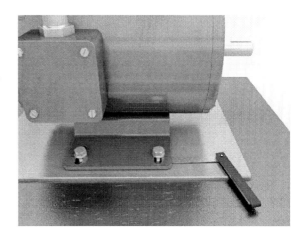

Set the machine in place but do not tighten the mounting bolt nuts.

Attempt to pass a thin feeler gauge underneath each of the four feet. A foot is soft if the feeler gauge passes beneath most of it and only contacts a small point or one edge.

If the feeler passes beneath a foot, determine the exact amount of gap beneath the foot with a feeler gauge and place this amount of shims beneath that foot. Consider this the initial soft foot correction.

Final Soft Foot

Tighten the motor mounting nuts. Place the stem of a dial indicator vertically above the foot that is to be checked for a soft foot. Set the dial indicator to zero.

Completely loosen the mounting bolt nuts on that foot only. Watch the dial indicator for foot movement during the loosening process.

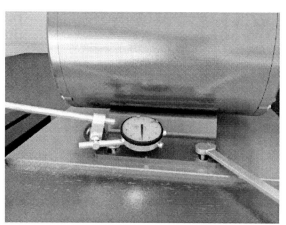

Retighten the hold-down nut and repeat the entire process once more to be sure no movement is present.

Move the dial indicator and holder to the next foot to be checked and repeat the process. Remember to securely tighten all other feet when checking a foot for a soft foot condition.

If one of the feet raises from the base more than 0.002 inch for large motors or 0.010 inch for small motors when the hold-down nut is loosened, place an amount of shim stock equal to the amount of deflection shown on the dial indicator beneath the foot.

If more than one foot rises, shim the one with the most rise. Repeat this process for each machine foot.

Description of Shaft Run-Out

Another step to perform as part of the motor mounting process is to check the motor shaft for run-out and end float.

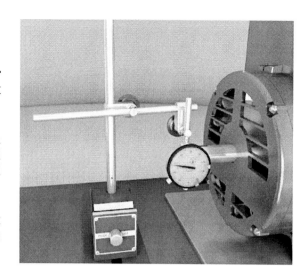

Check run-out by placing a dial indicator on the shaft and rotating the shaft. The total variation in the reading is called the total indicator reading (TIR).

The run-out is one half of the TIR. Do not use the motor if the run-out exceeds 0.002 inch.

High run-out means either the motor shaft is bent or the bearings are worn. Run-out can be checked at any time during the installation process.

Description of End Float

Also, check the motor for end float or end play. End float is the amount of free movement the shaft can make along its axis.

If end float is excessive, use of the motor can cause misalignment.

Check end float by placing an indicator on the end of the shaft and move the shaft in and out. Compare the end float to the manufacturer's specifications. A typical end float is 0.001 inch, but can vary.

Importance of Leveling the Motor

It is important in most cases to level the electric motor drive before beginning the alignment of the motor with the components it is going to drive.

Leveling the motor makes it easier to align the motor later because any additional shims needed to raise the motor to the height of the other equipment can be added equally to each foot.

Leveling the Motor

Leveling a motor end to end is a five-step process.

Step 1

Place a small level on top of the motor shaft.

Step 2

Place one or more of the leaves of a feeler gauge under one end of the level, whichever ones are necessary to make the horizontal bubble centered.

Step 3

Calculate the ratio of the distance between the centers of the motor mounting bolts and the length between one end of the level and the edge of the feeler gauge leaf.

Length Ratio Formula

$$R = \frac{L_B}{L_E}$$

Where:

L_E = Effective Level Length (in)

L_B = Mounting Bolts Center Distance (in)

R = Length Ratio

Step 4

Multiply the feeler gauge leaf thickness by the length ratio of step three.

Shim Thickness Needed Formula

$$T_S = R \times T_F$$

Where:

T_S = Shim Thickness Needed (in)

R = Shim Ratio

T_F = Thickness of the Feeler Gauge (in)

Step 5

Shim under the low end of the motor by an amount equal to your calculation in step 4.

Leveling Process

This leveling process does not precisely level the motor, but it "roughs in" the position of the motor to make it easier when you later align it with another piece of equipment.

The leveling process just described is also used to level entire machines, machine foundations, and bedplates.

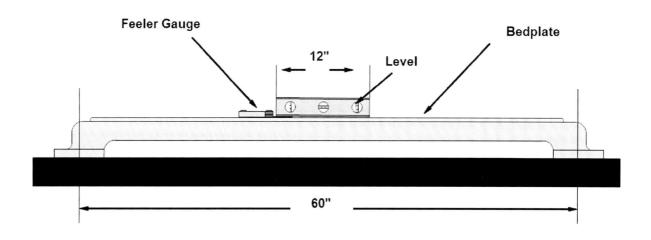

Mounting and Leveling the Motor

Eight steps are required to level a motor, including checking for soft foot and run-out.

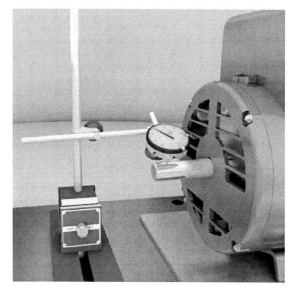

Step 1

Clean the motor base, shims, and mounting surface of all burrs, rust, and dirt.

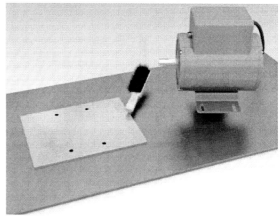

Step 2

Position the motor over the mounting holes on the bedplate.

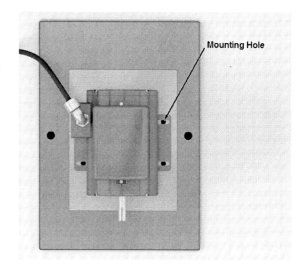

Step 3

Check and correct for the initial soft foot condition.

Step 4

Attach the fasteners with washers and nuts. Tighten them down using a criss-cross pattern until the bolts are tight.

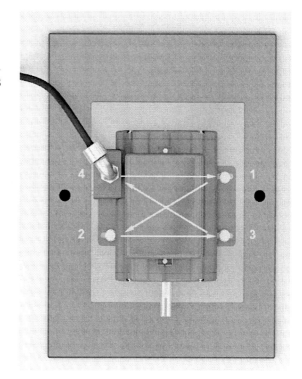

Step 5

Check for and correct the final soft foot condition.

Step 6

Tighten the bolts again in a criss-cross pattern.

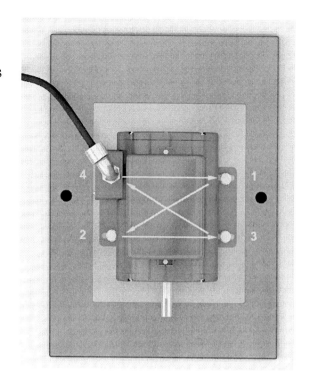

Step 7

Level the motor end to end.

Step 8

Check the motor for run-out and end float.

Segment 4 Shaft Speed Measurement

Objective 14 Describe Two Methods of Measuring Motor Shaft Speed and Give an Application

The Definition of Motor Speed

Motor speed is the measure of how fast the motor shaft is rotating. For example, the motor shaft shown here is turning at the rate of one revolution per second.

The rotational speed of a motor is usually given in units of revolutions per minute (rpm). Therefore, the speed of this motor is sixty revolutions per minute (60 rpm).

Two Types of Tachometers

Instruments designed to measure motor speed are called tachometers. There are several types of tachometers, each based on a different method of measurement.

Two common types of tachometers are:

• Contact Tachometer
• Photo Tachometer

Contact Tachometer

The contact tachometer works much the same as a car speedometer. It has an internal gear system that converts the rotating motion of a shaft into a reading shown on the tachometer.

To take a reading with the contact tachometer, hold the rubber-tipped shaft against the spinning motor shaft. This causes the tachometer shaft to spin at the same speed as the motor shaft. The reading on the tachometer will then indicate the rotational speed.

Photo Tachometer

The photo tachometer uses a beam of light pointed at a piece of reflective tape on the motor's shaft. The photo tachometer counts the number of times the tape passes through the light.

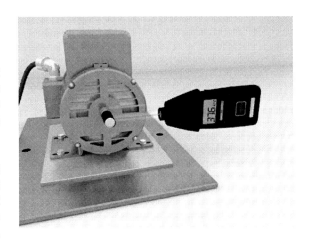

Once the photo tachometer determines the speed, it is shown on the display. This method has an advantage over the contact tachometer because you do not come in direct contact with the motor shaft. However, some models have attachments that enable you to take direct readings if necessary.

Module 2 Key Fasteners

Segment 1   Keyseat Fasteners

Objective 1   Describe the Function and Operation of a Key Fastener

Function of a Key Fastener

A key fastener secures the shaft to other devices such as couplings, sheaves, and gears. Its job is to make sure that the drive shaft and the driven component are locked together and do not slip on each other.

A key fastener consists of up to three parts.

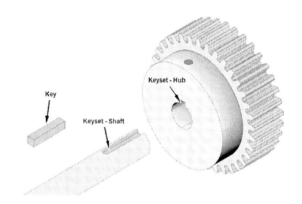

Key

A key is simply a piece of metal that is snugly fitted between two grooves, which are machined in a shaft and the hub of a component to which it is to be connected.

Keyseat - Shaft

The groove in the drive shaft is called a keyseat.

Keyseat - Hub

The groove in the hub is also known as a keyseat or sometimes a keyway.

In many cases, hubs have one or more set screws that can apply extra force to the key to lock the hub in place.

Objective 2   Describe the Construction of Six Types of Keys and Give an Application of Each

Six Types of Keys

There are many types of keys used in industry. Each key has a certain shape or design determined by ease of use, cost, or its ability to hold a high load.

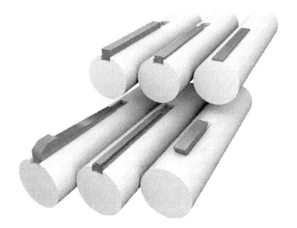

- Square
- Rectangular
- Saddle
- Gib Head
- Offset
- Woodruff

Square

The square key is the most widely used because it is easy to make and provides a strong connection. Its cross section is square and its length can be either tapered or parallel.

The parallel type is the most commonly used. The tapered type uses a wedging action to keep the key in place.

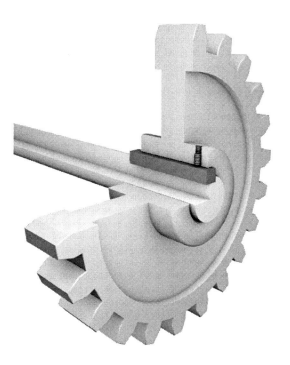

Rectangular

This key looks like a square key except that its width is greater than a square key. It can also be a parallel or tapered type.

The rectangular key has greater shear strength because of its larger cross-sectional area. Rectangular keys are preferred for shaft sizes greater than 6-1/2 inches. For smaller sizes, a square key is preferred.

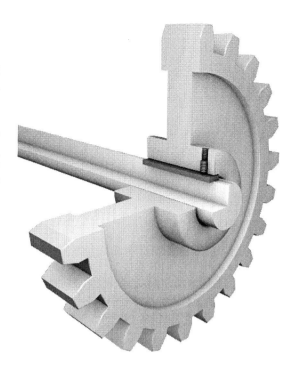

Saddle

The saddle key is used where there is no keyseat of any kind. These are used in light duty applications.

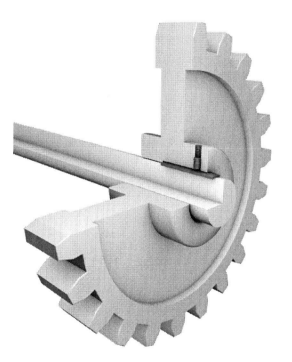

Gib Head

The gib head key is a tapered square key with a head on it. The head provides a way to easily remove the key if only one side of the assembly is accessible.

A tapered key without a head is a plain taper key.

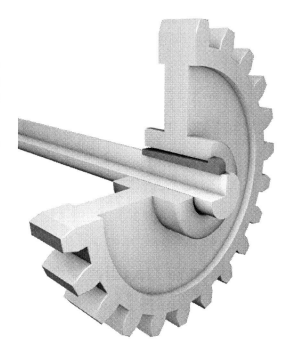

Offset

The offset or step key is a type of square key that has a different width on one side of the key. This allows the key to connect a coupling hub and shaft that have different keyseat sizes.

It is also used for repair and salvage of keyseats that have become larger through wear.

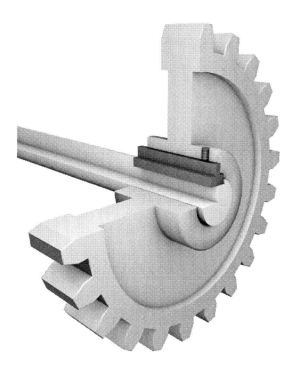

Woodruff

The woodruff key is shaped like a half moon. It is used for light duty applications because it gives more holding strength (more shear area) without requiring a large portion of the shaft to have a key seat machined in it.

It is also used with tapered shafts because it reduces the tendency of the key to tip when a load is applied.

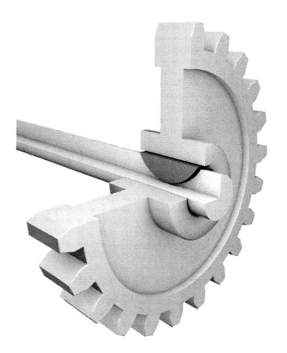

Objective 3   Describe How Keys and Keyseats Are Specified

Key and Keyseat Specifications

Keys are made from standard stock sizes which are available from machine parts suppliers. Suppliers use the following features to specify keys and keyseats:

- Nominal Width & Height
- Width & Height Tolerance
- Length
- Material Type

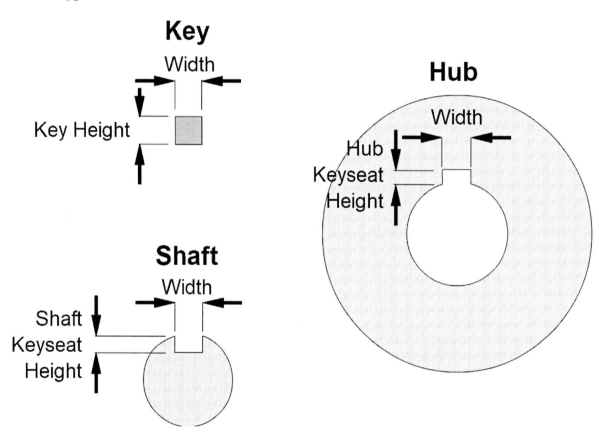

Nominal Width of Keys and Keyseats

The nominal width is the width of both the key stock and the keyseat, without accounting for tolerance. Key stock is available in a variety of standard widths and is usually selected from a table like the one shown.

The manufacturer of the equipment normally machines the keyseats into the shaft and hub. However, many drive components are also available with no keyseats to allow the user to custom machine the keyseats.

Nominal Shaft Diameter			Nominal Key Size		Nominal Keyseat Depth	
			Height, H		H/2	
Over	To (Incl.)	Width, W	Square	Rectangular	Square	Rectangular
5/16	7/16	3/32	3/32	....	3/64	....
7/16	9/16	1/8	1/8	3/32	1/16	3/64
9/16	7/8	3/16	3/16	1/8	3/32	1/16
7/8	1-1/4	1/4	1/4	3/16	1/8	3/32
1-1/4	1-3/4	5/16	5/16	1/4	5/32	1/8
1-3/8	2	3/8	3/8	1/4	3/16	1/8
1-3/4	2-1/4	1/2	1/2	3/8	....	3/16
2-1/4	2-3/4	5/8	5/8	7/16	5/16	7/32
2-3/4	3-1/4	3/4	3/4	1/2	3/8	1/4
3-1/4	3-3/4	7/8	7/8	5/8	7/16	5/16
3-3/4	4-1/2	1	1	3/4	1/2	3/8
4-1/2	5-1/2	1-1/4	1-1/4	7/8	5/8	7/16
5-1/2	6-1/2	1-1/2	1-1/2	1	3/4	1/2
6-1/2	7-1/2	3-3/4	1-3/4	1-1/2*	7/8	3/4
7-1/2	9	2	2	1-1/2	1	3/4
9	11	2-1/2	2-1/2	1-3/4	1-1/4	7/8

All dimensions are given in inches. For larger shaft sizes, see ANSI Standard. Square keys preferred for shaft diameters above heavy line; rectangular keys, below.
* Some key standards show 1-1/4 inches; preferred height is 1-1/2 inches.

Nominal Height of Keys and Keyseats

The nominal key height is the height of the key stock, without accounting for tolerance. For a square key, the nominal height is the same as the nominal width.

The nominal keyseat height, however, is not the same as the key height. The nominal keyseat height is normally chosen to be half the key height because the key must extend into the keyseats of both the hub and the shaft.

In the case of a square key, the nominal height is the same as the nominal width.

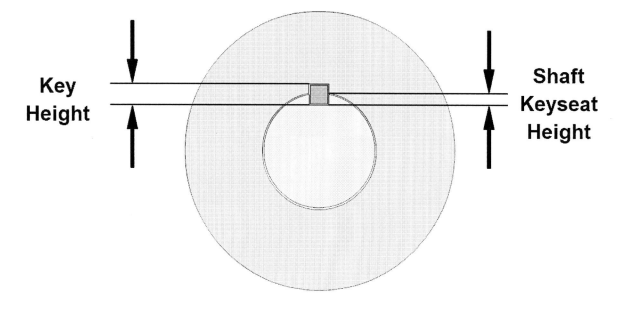

Width and Height Tolerances

The width and height tolerances are the allowable variations of the width and height dimensions of the key and keyseat from the nominal width or height as shown in the table.

Width tolerances are necessary to avoid a fit that is too loose or too tight between the key and keyseat. A loose fit can cause shearing and a tight fit can cause failure due to stress cracks in the shaft or hub.

Nominal Shaft Diameter			Nominal Key Size		Nominal Keyseat Depth	
			Height, H		H/2	
Over	To (Incl.)	Width, W	Square	Rectangular	Square	Rectangular
5/16	7/16	3/32	3/32	....	3/64	....
7/16	9/16	1/8	1/8	3/32	1/16	3/64
9/16	7/8	3/16	3/16	1/8	3/32	1/16
7/8	1-1/4	1/4	1/4	3/16	1/8	3/32
1-1/4	1-3/4	5/16	5/16	1/4	5/32	1/8
1-3/8	2	3/8	3/8	1/4	3/16	1/8
1-3/4	2-1/4	1/2	1/2	3/8	....	3/16
2-1/4	2-3/4	5/8	5/8	7/16	5/16	7/32
2-3/4	3-1/4	3/4	3/4	1/2	3/8	1/4
3-1/4	3-3/4	7/8	7/8	5/8	7/16	5/16
3-3/4	4-1/2	1	1	3/4	1/2	3/8
4-1/2	5-1/2	1-1/4	1-1/4	7/8	5/8	7/16
5-1/2	6-1/2	1-1/2	1-1/2	1	3/4	1/2
6-1/2	7-1/2	3-3/4	1-3/4	1-1/2*	7/8	3/4
7-1/2	9	2	2	1-1/2	1	3/4
9	11	2-1/2	2-1/2	1-3/4	1-1/4	7/8

All dimensions are given in inches. For larger shaft sizes, see ANSI Standard. Square keys preferred for shaft diameters above heavy line; rectangular keys, below.
* Some key standards show 1-1/4 inches; preferred height is 1-1/2 inches.

Tolerance Classifications

The tolerances of the key and keyseat can have one of two types of fits as determined by ANSI: either class 1 or class 2.

Class 1 is a looser fit than class 2. In a normal application, the fit you used with a key should be a class 1 fit so it will be the only fit discussed.

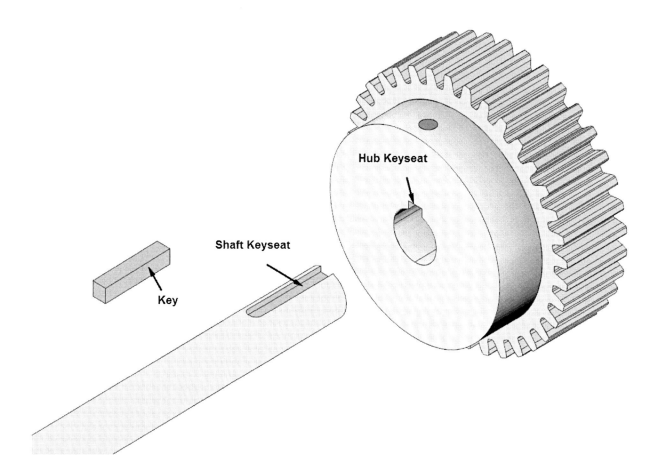

Class 1 Fit

A class 1 fit is a type of clearance fit called a sliding fit. This means that there is a slight clearance between the key and the keyseat (typically 0.001 to 0.002 inch clearance) but the clearance should not be detectable by touch.

The key should be able to be pushed into the keyseat with your thumb.

The class 1 tolerances for square and rectangular keys and keyseats for various sizes of shafts are given in the table shown. This table, as well as the one for a class 2 fit, are in the Machinery's Handbook. An example of what they will look like is provided here in the table.

You should use the fit table to determine the proper key for a given keyseat.

Class I Fit for Parallel Keys									
Type of Key	Key Width		Side Fit			Top and Bottom Fit			
			Width Tolerance		Fit Range*	Depth Tolerance			Fit Range*
	Over	To (Incl.)§	Key	Keyseat		Key	Keyseat	Hub Keyseat	
Square	—	1/2	+0.000 -0.002	+0.002 -0.000	0.004 CL 0.000	+0.000 -0.002	+0.000 -0.015	+0.010 -0.000	0.032 CL 0.005 CL
	1/2	3/4	+0.000 -0.002	+0.003 -0.000	0.005 CL 0.000	+0.000 -0.002	+0.000 -0.015	+0.010 -0.000	0.032 CL 0.005 CL
	3/4	1	+0.000 -0.003	+0.003 -0.000	0.006 CL 0.000	+0.000 -0.003	+0.000 -0.015	+0.010 -0.000	0.033 CL 0.005 CL
	1	1-1/2	+0.000 -0.003	+0.004 -0.000	0.007 CL 0.000	+0.000 -0.003	+0.000 -0.015	+0.010 -0.000	0.033 CL 0.005 CL
	1-1/2	2-1/2	+0.000 -0.004	+0.004 -0.000	0.008 CL 0.000	+0.000 -0.004	+0.000 -0.015	+0.010 -0.000	0.034 CL 0.005 CL
	2-1/2	3-1/2	+0.000 -0.006	+0.004 -0.000	0.010 CL 0.000	+0.000 -0.006	+0.000 -0.015	+0.010 -0.000	0.036 CL 0.005 CL

All dimensions are given in inches.
*Limits of variation. CL = Clearance

Matching Keys and Keyseats

Key tolerances are either:

- Undersize
- Oversize
- Over/Undersize

Keyseats are machined into the shaft and hub with class 1 tolerance, so that there is a clearance fit. Many times the manufacturer of the shaft or hub machines the keyseat, so your only job is to select the key stock tolerance.

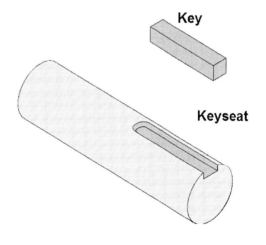

Undersize

Undersize key stock fits the tolerance specification shown for a class 1 fit. It has a zero upper tolerance.

For example, a typical undersize tolerance is 0.000 to -0.001 inch. This tolerance type is the most commonly used because it ensures that there is always some clearance.

The undersize tolerance is also called a negative tolerance or minus tolerance.

The text in red is the width desired for the key or keyseat.

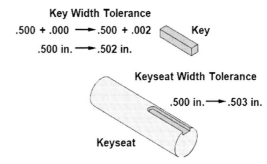

Key Width Tolerance
.500 - .001 → .500 + .000   Key
.499 in. → .500 in.

Keyseat Width Tolerance
.500 in. → .503 in.
Keyseat

Oversize

An oversize key tolerance means that the lower tolerance is zero. A typical oversize tolerance is +0.002 to 0.000 inch.

Oversize key stock is used when the keyseats are worn and have therefore become larger than the normal specification allows.

The oversize key allows the shaft to still be used. Another term used for this tolerance type is a plus tolerance.

The text in red is the width desired for the key or keyseat.

Key Width Tolerance
.500 + .000 → .500 + .002   Key
.500 in. → .502 in.

Keyseat Width Tolerance
.500 in. → .503 in.
Keyseat

Over/Undersize

Over/undersize tolerance means that there is both an upper and lower tolerance. A typical example is +0.0005 to -0.0005 inch.

This tolerance works best when you want a tighter-than-normal fit. An example of an application is with a reversing motor.

The text in red is the width desired for the key or keyseat.

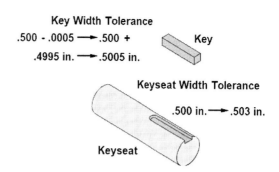

Key and Keyseat Length

Another feature that must be specified is the length of the key.

While the nominal length of the key is important, it is not a critical dimension. The general guideline is to make the key long enough to fit flush on one side of the hub and a little shorter than the length of the keyseat on the shaft to ensure that the key cannot slide around in the keyseat.

Keys are available in various lengths. However, keys are normally cut to length from longer lengths of key stock, such as a typical stock length of 12 inches.

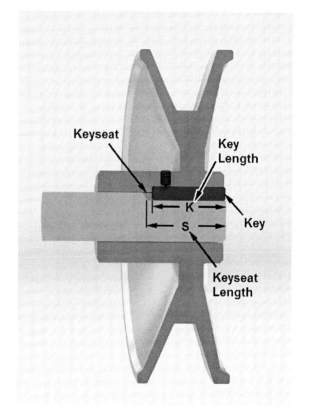

Key Stock Material Type

Keys are purposely chosen to be of a softer material than the shaft so that they will shear first if the shaft is overloaded.

Common key materials include:

- Cold rolled steel, e.g. C1018
- Zinc-plated cold rolled steel
- High carbon steel, e.g. C1095
- Brass

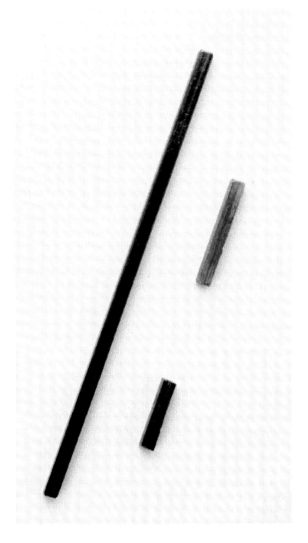

The most common material is cold rolled steel. This material may be zinc plated for corrosion resistance.

Stainless steel, typically 316 or 18-8, is common for the same reason. In marine applications, brass is also used.

For higher load applications, where tighter tolerances and higher strength are needed, a high carbon steel can be used. This steel is often annealed to make it easier to machine and has a tighter size tolerance.

Segment 2   Key Assembly

Objective 4   Describe How to Measure the Actual Size of a Key and Keyseat

Sizing Keys and Keyseats

Selecting the right size for a key is very important. Accurate measurement of the keyseat and the right size key stock are crucial in selecting the proper key.

There are three measuring tools that are used to measure the key and keyseat.

- Dial Caliper
- Micrometer
- Rule

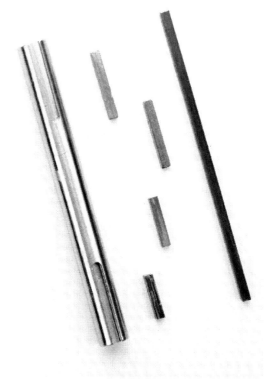

Dial Caliper

The dial caliper has the ability to measure the inside width of a keyseat and the depth of the keyseat.

These measurements allow you to determine the width and height of the key.

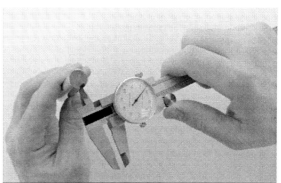

Micrometer

Either the micrometer or the caliper is suitable to measure both the width and height of the key stock used to make the key. The micrometer is a more accurate measuring device than the dial caliper and is more commonly used for this application.

A key stock that is purchased from a supplier has a specific tolerance. For example, square key stock (e.g. zinc-plated, cold-drawn C1018 steel key stock) is typically sold with a tolerance of +0.003, 0.000 in.

Therefore, it is usually only necessary to verify that the nominal size of the key stock is correct because the tolerance of the key stock has already been specified.

Rule

A rule measures the length of a keyseat. This measurement is difficult using a micrometer or the dial caliper.

Because the length is not critical, a rule is the easiest and quickest method of determining the keyseat's approximate length.

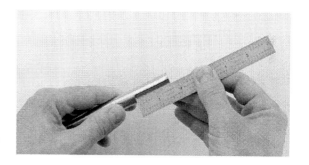

Objective 5   Describe Six Types of Set Screws

Six Types of Set Screws

A set screw is a threaded fastener used to hold components together. These fasteners generally do not have a head.

There are various types of set screws available.

- Cup Point
- Flat Point
- Dog Point
- Oval Point
- Cone Point
- Soft Tipped

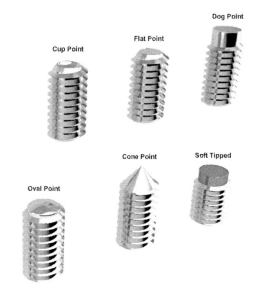

Cup Point

Cup point set screws have a dished out area on their tip. This cup bites into the shaft for maximum locking strength.

Flat Point

Flat point set screws are used because they offer the least amount of shaft deformation. They are typically used on frequently dismantled components.

Dog Point

Dog point set screws have a point that fits into a hole in the shaft. This provides not only locking strength, but also provides precise locating of the components in reference to each other.

Oval Point

Oval point set screws do not create excessive indentations in the shaft. However, they are best when the set screw will contact the shaft at an angle.

Cone Point

Cone point set screws are used for permanent mounting of components on shafts. The point bites into the shaft to create a high axial and torsional locking strength.

Soft Tipped

Soft tipped set screws have a different material on the point, typically nylon and brass. This material conforms to the shape of the shaft. This provides adequate locking strength for many applications and prevents damaging or scarring of soft shafts.

Objective 6   Describe How to Assemble a Hub to a Shaft Using a Key Fastener

Assembling a Shaft and Hub with a Key Fastener

Assembling a shaft and hub with a key fastener is a very easy task if the components are sized correctly.

- Step 1: Check the Hub
- Step 2: Clean the Keyseats
- Step 3: Slide the Key onto the Shaft Keyseat
- Step 4: Insert Key into the Hub Keyseat
- Step 5: Re-Insert Key into the Shaft Keyseat
- Step 6: Align the Hub and Shaft
- Step 7: Slide the Hub onto the Shaft
- Step 8: Tighten the Set Screw

Step 1: Check the Hub

Check to see if the hub has a set screw hole drilled in its side. A set screw can provide an extra holding force on the key to hold it in position. If there is a set screw, make sure to back it out so that it is not extending into the shaft hole.

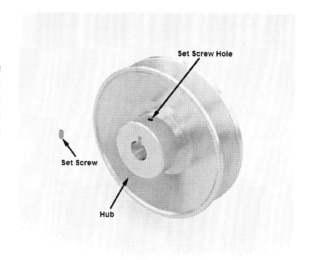

Step 2: Clean the Keyseats

Clean the shaft keyseat and the hub keyseat with a wire brush to make sure that no dirt or burrs are in the keyseats.

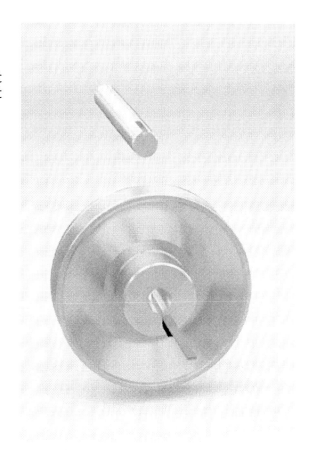

Step 3: Slide the Key onto the Shaft Keyseat

Slide the key onto the keyseat of the shaft. The key should fit into the keyseat without forcing it. If it is too tight, take it out and measure it to see which part is out of tolerance. You can either replace the key, machine the keyseat, or sand the key.

Sanding the key is normally not recommended because it is difficult to sand it evenly. If you choose to sand it, use a belt sander, not a grinder.

Also, check the key for play when it is in the keyseat by wiggling it. There should be no play. If there is, replace the key.

Step 4: Insert Key into the Hub Keyseat

Remove the key from the shaft keyseat and insert it into the hub keyseat. It also should slide in without forcing it and have no play.

Step 5: Re-Insert Key into the Shaft Keyseat

Remove the key from the hub and insert into the shaft keyseat. Line it up flush with the end of the shaft.

Step 6: Align the Hub and Shaft

Pick up the hub in your hand and line it up in front of the shaft so that the hub's keyseat is in line with the key on the shaft.

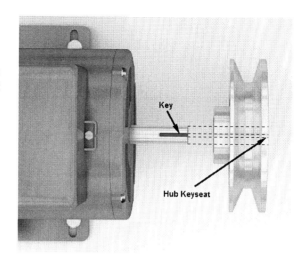

Step 7: Slide the Hub onto the Shaft

Slide the hub onto the shaft until the end of the hub is flush with the end of the shaft. The hub should slide without using tools. If it doesn't, pull it off and check the dimensions.

Step 8: Tighten the Set Screw

Tighten the set screw onto the key. Sometimes you may use two set screws to keep the first one from backing out when the shaft is turning.

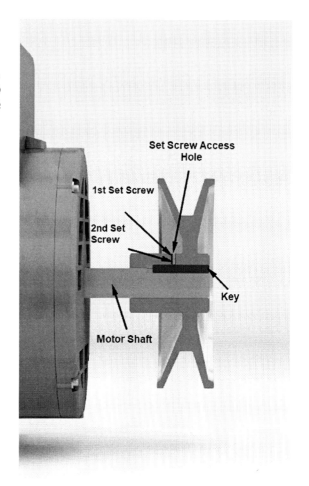

Hub Removal

The best way to remove a hub from a shaft is to use a bearing puller. This unit pushes on the end of the shaft while it pulls on the hub. This method will remove the hub without damaging the components.

Another method of removing a hub is to use a key punch and soft hammer to tap the key out. The hub is then removed by hand. However, a hammer should never knock out the hub directly. This will destroy the hub.

Segment 3   Torque and Power Measurement

Objective 7   Describe Two Methods of Loading a Mechanical Drive System

Loading a Mechanical Drive System

In some cases, an external device loads certain mechanical devices in order to measure the performance characteristics at various loads.

There are two common methods used to load a mechanical drive system:

• Prony Brake
• Dynamometer

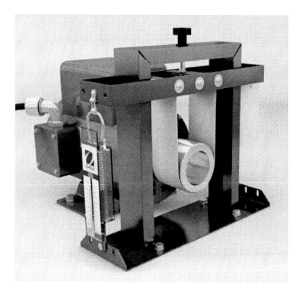

Prony Brake

The prony brake is one device that is used to load a motor. This device also has the ability to tell you how much load is applied to the motor.

The prony brake drum couples to the motor shaft and rests inside a canvas friction belt. As the canvas belt tightens against the brake drum using the wingnut, the load on the motor is increased. This applies a force to the pivot arm.

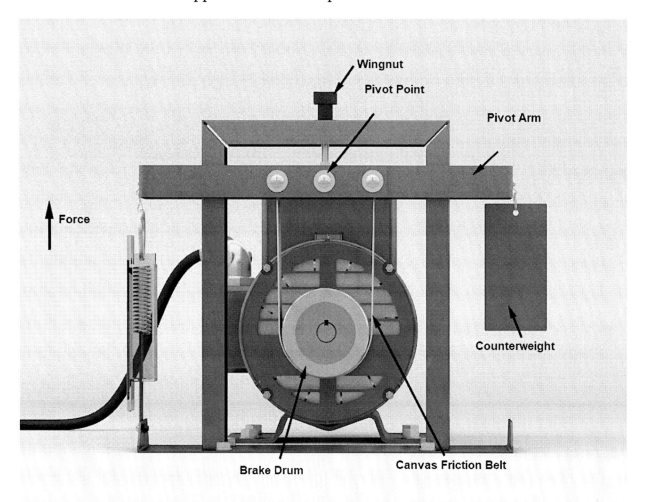

The force is measured by a spring scale that is placed at a specific distance from the center of the motor shaft. This is the radius distance. You can then use the force reading from the scale and the radius distance to calculate the torque.

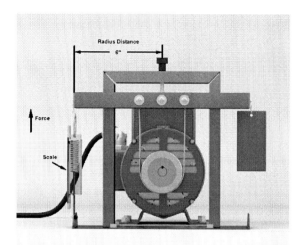

Dynamometer

A dynamometer is another type of device that places a load on a motor and measures the amount of power that the motor can produce. Race car builders use dynamometers to tune their engines.

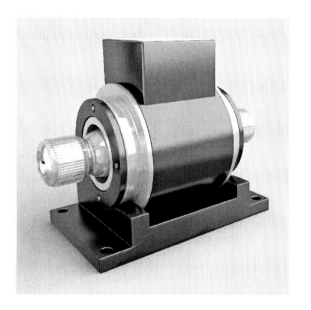

Objective 8   Describe How to Calculate Rotary Mechanical Power

Define Rotary Power

Rotary mechanical power is defined as the rate or speed at which the rotating power transmission system turns the load. Since work is defined as Force x Distance, work in a rotating system is actually torque.

This means that the power output at a motor's shaft is found by multiplying the torque by the speed (rate) as shown.

Rotary Power Formula

$$P = T_S \times S_S$$

Where:

P = Rotary Power (hp)

T_S = Shaft Torque (ft-lb or N-m)

S_S = Shaft Speed (rpm)

Units of Rotary Power

The units of rotary power are expressed in horsepower (hp) in the US customary system and kilowatts (kW) in the Systems International (SI) system. They are calculated as shown in the formulas.

Motor Power-US Customary

$$P_O = \frac{T \times S}{5{,}252}$$

Where:

P_O = Output Power (hp)

T = Torque (ft-lb)

S = Speed (rpm)

Motor Power-SI

$$P_O = \frac{T \times S}{9{,}549}$$

Where:

P_O = Output Power (kW)

T = Torque (N-m)

S = Speed (rpm)

Segment 4   Mechanical Efficiency

Objective 9   Describe How to Calculate Mechanical Efficiency and Explain Its Importance

Define Mechanical Efficiency

One of the problems with power transmission equipment of any kind is that the power output is always less than the power input. This is because there are frictional effects in the transmission that cause some of the power to be lost to heat.

The ratio of the Power Out to the Power In is the Power Efficiency. If it is describing the power lost through a mechanical drive system, it is the Mechanical Power Efficiency. It can be calculated as shown in this formula.

Mechanical Power Efficiency

$$E_M = \left(\frac{P_o}{P_i} \right) \times 100$$

Where:

E_M = Mechanical efficiency (%)

P_o = Output power (hp or kW)

P_i = Input power (hp or kW)

Measuring Mechanical Efficiency

The mechanical power efficiency is important to any machine. The goal of a designer is to make it as high as possible, so that the machine uses as little energy as possible to perform its task.

How maintenance technicians align and lubricate a machine also affects its efficiency. The mechanical efficiency will decrease as the machine wears. This means that monitoring the efficiency will tell you when a machine needs servicing.

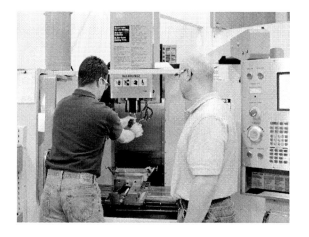

The mechanical efficiency of a power transmission can be determined by measuring the shaft speed and torque at the input and the output.

In some cases, the power loss may occur because of a loss of speed due to slip in the drive components. In others, the power loss occurs by lost torque from friction. Lost torque is the most common source of power loss.

Applications of Mechanical Efficiency

In actual application, measuring the mechanical power at either the input shaft or the output shaft is hard to do because it is not easy to measure the torque.

The torque can be measured by using a torque transducer, an electronic device that attaches to the shaft, or a dynamometer.

In most cases, you can more easily monitor the efficiency of the system by measuring the electric power drawn by the motor. If it increases over time, you know that the mechanical drive is losing efficiency.

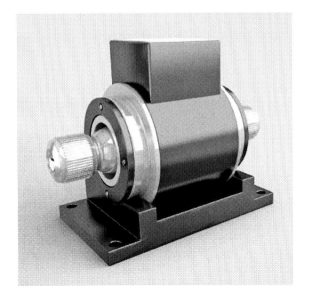

Objective 10 Describe Two Methods of Measuring Shaft Torque and Give an Application of Each

Measuring Shaft Torque

Measuring the load on the mechanical drive system is useful because it allows you to determine how the system is operating. A problem in the drive system will often cause a change in the load. For example, excessive tension in a V-belt will cause a higher load.

These are two methods you can use to measure the load on a shaft:

• Current Measurement
• Torque Transducer

Current Measurement

Torque is related to the electrical current supplied to the motor. As motor torque increases, so does electrical current.

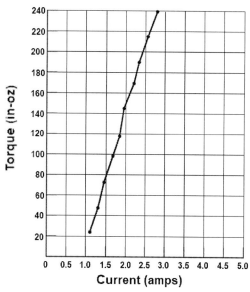

Most motor manufacturers have already tested this relationship and include a graph with the specifications of the motor that shows the torque vs. current characteristics. Torque is determined by comparing measured current to the graph.

For example, from the torque vs. current graph shown here you can see that if the measured current is 2 amps, the torque delivered by the motor is approximately 150 in-oz.

Current measurement often is used to measure motor torque in the field because the motor is already connected to a load.

Torque Transducer

A torque transducer is a device that is directly coupled to the shaft and generates an electrical signal that an ammeter or controller receives.

The form of the signal is usually either a ±10 VAC or 4-20 mA signal. This signal is proportional to the torque.

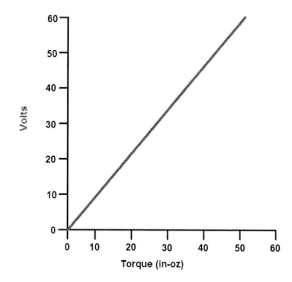

Measuring Electrical Current

Measuring the electric motor's input current is a way to monitor the efficiency of a mechanical drive system. As the efficiency decreases, the motor's current will increase. This shows that the load of the drive has increased.

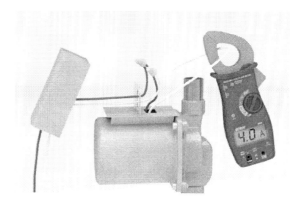

There are three methods by which motor current can be measured:

• Clamp-on ammeter
• Hand-held ammeter
• Built-in ammeter

Clamp-On Ammeters

A clamp-on ammeter can be opened and placed around a wire in which you want to measure the current.

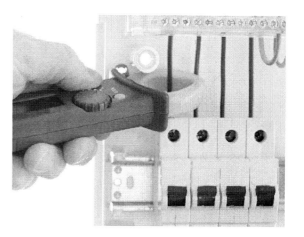

This is very convenient because it allows you to measure current without disconnecting the circuit to connect the meter in series.

This aspect is very important for AC power applications where the current level is often quite high and very dangerous.

Handheld Ammeter

A handheld ammeter is a meter in which metal probes must be in series with the circuit in order to read current. To read the current the circuit must be broken and the ammeter must be inserted.

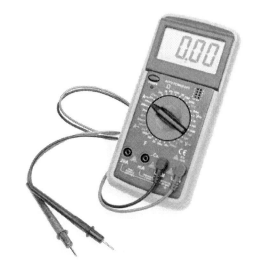

Precautions must be taken with a handheld ammeter. Placing the ammeter across a live component can short out the component, blow an ammeter fuse, or even cause the ammeter to explode.

These meters often come in the form of multimeters. Multimeters have the advantage of being able to measure voltage and resistance along with current.

Built-In Ammeters

Built-in ammeters are given their name since they are a permanent part of the circuit. Since they are built into the machine's panel they are also referred to as panel ammeters.

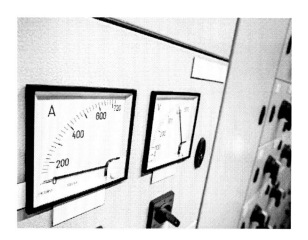

Built-in ammeters are used in applications where the current can be continually monitored.

Module 3 Power Transmission Systems

Segment 1   Introduction to Shafts

Objective 1   Describe the Function of a Shaft and Give an Application

The Definition of a Shaft

A shaft is a cylindrical piece of material, usually steel, that transmits mechanical power in the form of torque and rotating motion from one location to another.

The Operation of a Shaft

A shaft is a basic yet important component. Shafts transmit power to a location outside the machine, such as in an electrical motor or gas turbine.

Shafts can also be extensions to other shafts. An example of this is a drive shaft on a car, which transmits the power from the transmission in the front of the car to the differential gearbox in the rear.

An Application of a Shaft

Still, a third and very common application of a shaft is to provide a means of operating the working components of the machine. Shafts are attached to rotating members of machines to perform the work.

For example, a drill spindle consists basically of a shaft with a cutter tool attached to it, as shown here.

Another application is a case in which a roller is a part of the shaft as in a roller press or a papermaking machine.

Objective 2   List Four Types of Shaft Materials and Give an Application of Each

Choosing Shaft Material

Most machine shafts are made of some type of steel determined by the amount of load the shaft has to carry and the conditions of the work environment.

If you are replacing a shaft in a machine, make sure that you are using the same material. Do not assume that two materials that look the same are the same.

Four Types of Shaft Materials

These are some examples of common shaft materials:

• Cold Rolled Steel
• Hardened Steel
• Chrome Plated Steel
• Stainless Steel

Cold Rolled Steel

Cold rolled steel is the most common of all shaft materials because it is cheap and easy to machine.

It is available in different strengths according to its carbon content. Cold rolled steel is used in most applications.

Hardened Steel

Hardened steel is cold rolled steel that is heat-treated in some manner to increase its strength. It is used in heavy-duty applications such as high-speed drive shafts.

Chrome Plated Steel

Chrome plated steel is cold rolled or hardened steel that has been given a coating or plated with chrome.

Chrome is a metal that is resistant to rusting and other corrosive applications. It is often used on rollers in presses.

Stainless Steel

Stainless steel resists rusting and is very strong. It combines the features of hardened steel and chrome plating.

In fact, stainless steel has some chrome in it. Use a stainless steel shaft where you need resistance to a corrosive environment, a better surface finish, or a stronger surface than chrome plating can provide.

Applications of stainless steel include machines where the equipment must be washed often with cleaning fluids, which can cause chrome to flake off.

Other Types of Shaft Materials

In addition to these examples, shafts are made from many other types of materials.

If you are designing a machine that uses shafts, you must consider the cost of the material, ease of machining, size, and the type of duty.

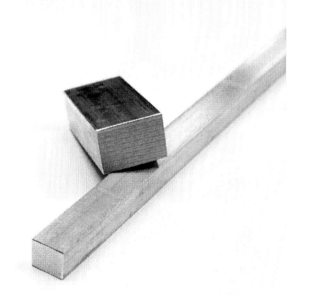

Objective 3   Describe How Shafts Are Specified

Shaft Specifications

Shaft specifications include the type of material, nominal diameter, diameter tolerance, straightness, and length.

Nominal Diameter	Diameter Tolerance (in.)			Straightness (in./ft)	
	Standard	Accuracy (Class "L")	Accuracy (Class "S")	Standard	Accuracy
1/4	0.251 to 0.249	0.2495 to 0.2490	0.2490 to 0.2485	Unspecified	0.001 to 0.002
3/8	0.3765 to 0.3735	0.3745 to 0.3740	0.3740 to 0.3735	Unspecified	0.001 to 0.002
1/2	0.5015 to 0.4985	0.4995 to 0.4990	0.4990 to 0.4985	Unspecified	0.001 to 0.002
5/8	0.627 to 0.623	0.6245 to 0.6240	0.6240 to 0.6235	Unspecified	0.001 to 0.002
3/4	0.7520 to 0.7480	0.7495 to 0.7490	0.7490 to 0.7485	Unspecified	0.001 to 0.002
1	1.002 to 0.998	0.9995 to 0.9990	0.9990 to 0.9985	Unspecified	0.001 to 0.002
1-1/4	1.2525 to 1.2475	1.2495 to 1.2490	1.2490 to 1.2485	Unspecified	0.001 to 0.002
1-1/2	1.5025 to 1.4975	1.4994 to 1.4989	1.4989 to 1.4984	Unspecified	0.001 to 0.002
2	2.0030 to 1.9970	1.9994 to 1.9987	1.9987 to 1.9980	Unspecified	0.001 to 0.002

Shaft Stock

Since a shaft is made from round stock material, approximate shaft diameters are usually the same as the common sizes of standard round stock. It is also important to determine the diameter tolerances and straightness the application requires.

Standard round stock is often not precise enough so designers select accuracy stock for most shaft applications.

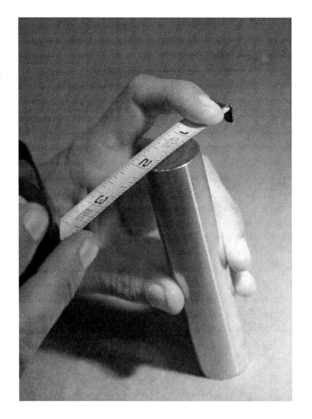

Accuracy Stock

Accuracy stock is precision ground to more exact tolerances than standard round stock.

Accuracy-type round stock is sold in standard lengths. Since shafts are usually shorter than the standard lengths, they are cut to length. This means the shaft length in a particular machine can be any length.

Segment 2 Introduction to Bearings

Objective 4   Describe the Function of a Bearing and Give an Application

The Function and an Application of Bearings

The function of a bearing is to support and guide a moving machine member with a minimum amount of friction.

To understand why bearings are needed, it is important to understand that a machine member often has loads acting on it in several directions.

Without bearings to hold the member in place, the loads would cause the member to move out of place and cause the machine to fail.

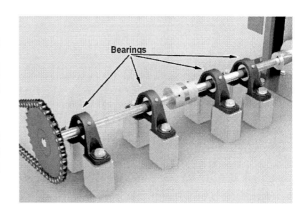

Bearings

Objective 5   Define Three Types of Bearing Loads and Give an Example of Each

Three Types of Bearing Loads

Bearings counteract three types of loads:

- Radial Load
- Thrust Load
- Combination

Radial Load

A radial or side load acts in a direction that is perpendicular to the axis of the shaft. For example, the force shown here on the bearings creates a radial load.

Radial bearings are bearings that carry a radial load. One source of radial load is the force from the weight of the power transmission component itself.

An example is the shaft shown here. The weight of the shaft creates a force that pulls downward on the radial bearings.

Tension or compression of the device the shaft is turning causes another type of radial load. Examples include the tension caused by a belt drive and the compression caused by a roller press.

These forces also create a radial load on the shaft.

Thrust Load

A thrust load acts in a direction parallel to the shaft axis and opposite to the direction of force transmission. These bearings are called thrust bearings.

The weight of the drive component can also cause a thrust load. One example is a machine element, such as a robot body or an index table, that must rotate parallel to the ground.

Another example of thrust load is the load created by a screw drive. As the screw drives the load, it creates a thrust load on the shaft in the opposite direction.

Combination

Many applications have a combination load with both a radial load and a thrust load. One example is the robot body like the one shown here.

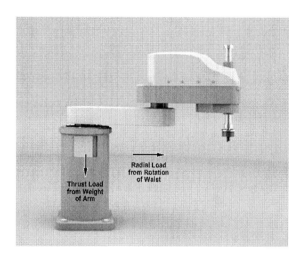

When the body rotates, the weight of the machine creates a radial load along with the thrust load. In fact, most loads that have a thrust load also have a radial load.

Objective 6 Describe How Bearings Are Positioned to Support a Load

Placement of the Load

No matter what the application, you can apply some basic concepts to understand where to place bearings in order to support a load. For radial loads, use at least two bearings to secure the position of the shaft.

Place the load between the two bearings or overhang it. An overhung load is often called a cantilever load.

Positioning Bearings

In some cases, the bearings are built into the machine rather than mounted externally. An example is an electric motor.

All electric motors have two bearings, one on each side of the housing, as shown here. These bearings support the motor's rotor and shaft.

Electric motors can also support an external radial load. This permits a mechanical member to be attached to the shaft without the use of external bearings.

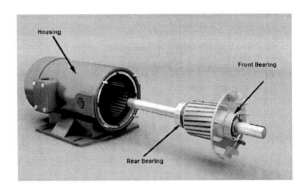

In contrast, thrust loads only need one bearing. Place this bearing anywhere on the shaft in a way such that it can counteract the direction of the thrust load.

Objective 7   Describe the Operation of Two Categories of Bearings and Give an Application of Each

Two Categories of Bearings

There are two major categories of bearings used in industry:

• Plain Bearings
• Anti-Friction Bearings

Plain Bearings

A plain bearing is a type of bearing in which the surface of the moving machine component slides over the bearing surface, separated only by a lubrication film.

Plain bearings are designed to support either radial loads or axial (thrust) loads. Journal bearings are radial load plain bearings for shafts. One application is on the crankshaft of a car engine.

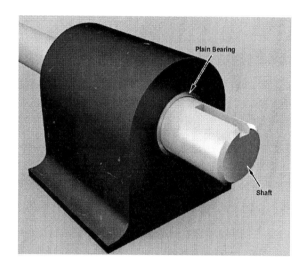

Anti-Friction Bearings

Anti-friction bearings, unlike plain bearings, rotate with the moving machine component. This is accomplished by using rollers or balls that rotate within the bearing.

These rollers replace the function of the lubrication film of the plain bearing. However, anti-friction bearings must use lubrication between the rollers.

Objective 8 — Describe Two Methods of Mounting a Shaft Bearing and Give an Application of Each

Two Methods of Shaft Bearing Mounts

All bearings require a housing or mounting of some type to hold the bearing in place in the machine. Mount plain and anti-friction shaft bearings in one of two ways:

- Pillow Block Bearing Mount
- Flange Bearing Mount

Pillow Block Bearing Mount

A pillow block consists of a housing with two mounting feet oriented so that you can mount the shaft to a horizontal or angled surface. A pillow block can be designed as either a single assembly or a split assembly.

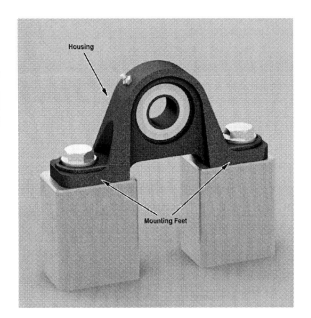

Flange Bearing Mount

A flange-type bearing mount consists of a housing with mounting feet that are oriented so that the shaft can be mounted to a surface that is perpendicular to the shaft.

Flanges have either two or four mounting holes. Some flanges are built into the housing of the machine itself, as is the case for an electric motor and pump.

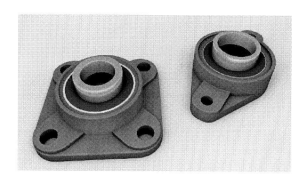

Shaft Bearing Mounts in Industry

Both the pillow block and flange bearing mounts are very popular and are common in industry.

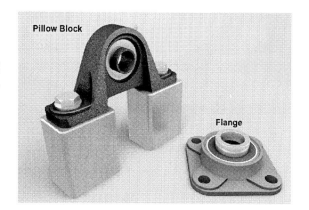

Segment 3 Introduction to Couplings

Objective 9   Describe the Function of a Coupling and Give an Application

Couplings Used to Connect a Shaft to a Driven Component

Couplings connect one shaft to another, such as connecting electric motors and other prime movers to driven devices like pumps and gear reducers.

Couplings Used to Extend Shafts

Couplings also can connect two shafts to create one long shaft. The coupling provides a secure method of transmitting the torque and speed from one shaft to another.

Although they appear to perform a rather simple task, there are many types of couplings, and their correct installation will greatly affect the mechanical efficiency and life of the system.

Objective 10 Describe the Function and Application of Four Categories of Mechanical Couplings

Four Categories of Mechanical Couplings

There are four general categories of mechanical couplings:

- Rigid Couplings
- Flexible Couplings
- Universal Joints
- Clutches

Rigid Couplings

Rigid couplings couple two shafts together rigidly so that the shafts act as a single continuous assembly. One type of rigid coupling is a flange coupling, as shown here.

Rigid couplings do not allow misalignment. They extend the length of a shaft in applications that need very long shaft lengths.

Rigid couplings sometimes connect motors to pumps. This is not recommended because any misalignment will cause the bearings to wear out quickly.

Flexible Couplings

Flexible couplings connect two shafts together and allow for some misalignment. In general, flexible couplings consist of two hubs and some type of flexible component that connects the two hubs together.

Flexible couplings are used in applications that require two independently supported coaxial shafts to be coupled together.

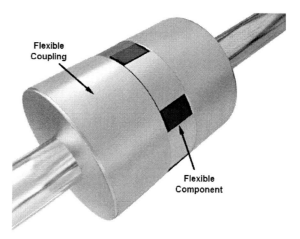

Independently supported shafts are very difficult to align perfectly. The flexible coupling allows enough misalignment to make the alignment process a practical task.

Applications that use flexible couplings include any electric motor or engine which must be coupled to a pump or gear reducer.

Universal Joints

The universal joint allows two shafts that are not coaxially aligned to be connected. The universal joint consists of one or two swivel connections that allow it to direct the shaft power to a shaft that is oriented at an angle to the driving shaft.

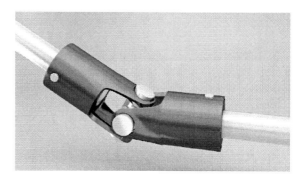

One example of an industrial application is a papermaking machine, which requires a motor to drive a roller that is offset from the motor shaft.

Clutches

The fourth category of couplings is clutches. Clutches are designed to allow two turning shafts to connect and disconnect from each other.

Clutches are used to start machines in an unloaded condition, prevent reverse rotation, and act as a safety device if the shaft torque overloads.

Objective 11 Describe the Operation of a Flexible Jaw Coupling

How the Flexible Jaw Coupling Works

The flexible jaw coupling is a type of flexible coupling that uses a rubber-like insert called a spider to connect the two hubs.

Each hub has jaws that mesh with the spider. When the driver coupling half rotates, its jaws press on the spider, which in turn presses on the jaws of the driven coupling half, causing it to turn.

The flexible jaw coupling is called an elastomer-in-compression, which is a member of the elastomeric family.

The hubs of a jaw coupling are constructed of aluminum, cast iron, or steel, depending on the power rating. They can be mounted with either a key fastener or bushing.

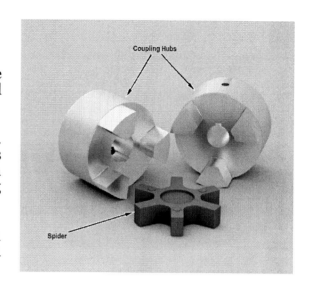

Composition of the Flexible Jaw Coupling

The spider can be made of Buna N (Nitrile) rubber, urethane, Hytril, or even metals such as bronze. They are usually designed as a one-piece construction, but can be supplied as pieces.

The advantage of this type of coupling is that it allows more misalignment than most flexible couplings because of the elastic properties of the elastomer spider. However, it is usually used for low to medium power or speed applications.

Other names for this coupling are a jaw and spider coupler, elastomeric jaw coupling, or simply a jaw coupling.

Segment 4   Shaft Alignment

Objective 12   Describe the Purpose of Shaft Alignment and Give Two Types of Misalignment

The Definition of Shaft Alignment

The centerlines of two shafts connected by a flexible coupling should be brought into line with each other before operating the shafts. This process is called shaft alignment.

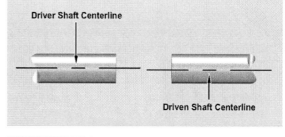

Types of Shaft Misalignment

Shaft alignment helps reduce vibration and extend the life of the couplings, bearings, and seals. Excessive vibration is known to be a main cause of early failure of equipment.

Shaft alignment corrects angular and parallel misalignment, which can appear anywhere in a 360° circle, but is usually measured on the horizontal and vertical planes.

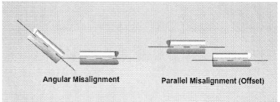

Objective 13 Describe a General Procedure for Shaft Alignment and Give Four Measurement Methods

The Process of Shaft Alignment

The general procedure for aligning two shafts is to check and correct for angular and parallel misalignment in the vertical and horizontal planes. Also, the coupling gap must be set when horizontal angular misalignment is corrected.

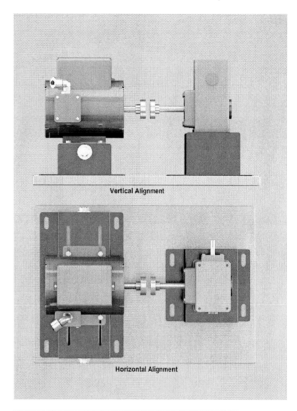

Five Checks and Corrections for Shaft Alignment

There are five checks and corrections for shaft alignment:

- Vertical Angular
- Vertical Parallel
- Horizontal Angular
- Coupling Gap
- Horizontal Parallel

Vertical Angular

To correct the vertical angular misalignment, add shims to the front or back of the motor, depending on the location of the misalignment.

If the gap between the couplings is greater at the top of the coupling, raise the back of the motor with shims. If the gap between the coupling hubs is greater at the bottom, raise the front of the motor with shims.

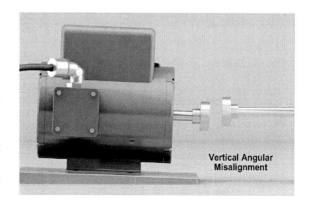

Vertical Angular Misalignment

Vertical Parallel

Vertical parallel alignment means to make the height of the two shafts the same.

To correct for vertical parallel misalignment, raise or lower the entire motor. Do this by adding or removing shims equally on all four motor feet, as shown here.

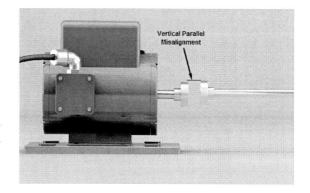

Vertical Parallel Misalignment

Horizontal Angular

To correct the horizontal angular misalignment, loosen the motor foot mount and slightly turn it in the direction that corrects the misalignment.

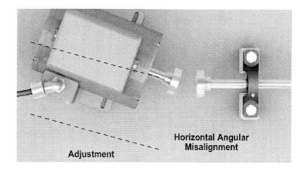

Adjustment

Horizontal Angular Misalignment

Coupling Gap

The coupling gap is the distance between the two coupling hubs. Set the coupling gap to the coupling manufacturer's specification.

This specification is designed to permit the coupling to assemble correctly. Since measuring horizontal angular misalignment means measuring the coupling gap, it is natural to adjust the gap at the same time. Simply angle the motor and move it forward or back.

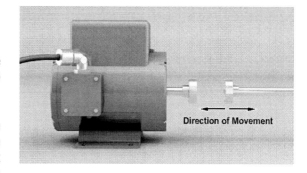

Direction of Movement

Horizontal Parallel

To correct for the horizontal parallel misalignment, loosen the motor foot mounts and move all four feet an equal amount, as shown here.

Correcting horizontal parallel alignment often upsets the horizontal angular alignment, so repeat horizontal angular alignment and horizontal parallel alignment procedures until the measurements are within the tolerances before tightening the bolts.

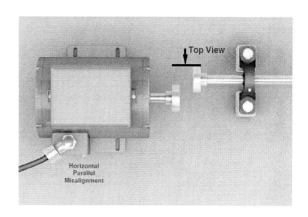

Explanation of Vertical Alignment Precedence

The two vertical alignment checks are done first because they require shims to be added to the motor's feet. Doing this last would upset the horizontal alignments.

For this reason, shaft alignment is also called coupling alignment. However, it is important to remember that the real goal is the alignment of the shafts.

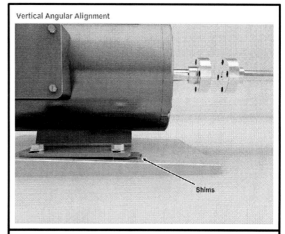

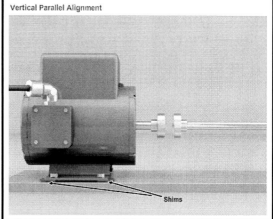

Four Methods of Measuring Misalignment

These are four methods of measuring the amount of misalignment, in order from least accurate to most accurate:

- Straight Edge and Feeler Gauge Method
- Face and Rim Method
- Reverse Indicator Method
- Laser Alignment

Straight Edge and Feeler Gauge Method

The straight edge and feeler gauge method is the least accurate method, but it is very quick. It is the method most people use to align a flexible jaw coupling since it can accept more misalignment than most other couplings.

Use the straight edge and feeler gauge method to make an initial rough alignment before performing further alignment methods.

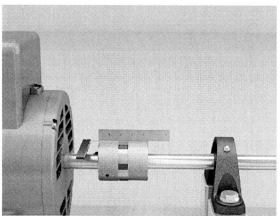

Deciding Which Machine to Move

Before beginning the alignment process, first decide which device is to move and which will remain in place. These will be referred to as the machine to be moved (MTBM) and the stationary machine.

Normally, the driver component is the MTBM and the driven component is the stationary machine. This is because the driver component is usually easier to move.

For example, a pump may not be easy to move if it has rigid plumbing attached to it.

Shimming the Machine to Move

Make sure that the height of the MTBM is slightly lower than the stationary machine. This is because the movable component will rise as it is shimmed during alignment.

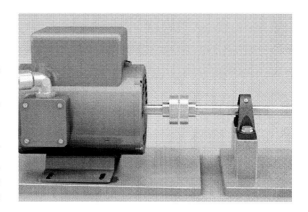

To accomplish this, the stationary component can be shimmed when it is mounted. A beginning height difference between the two shafts of 0.010 inch to 0.015 inch is good.

Couplings on the Machine to Move

Also, place the couplings on the shafts and move the MTBM into a position where the gap between the coupling hubs is approximately the amount recommended by the manufacturer.

This is normally done with the coupling hubs mounted flush with the ends of the shafts. One or both coupling hubs will then be secured in place on the shafts, depending on the coupling design and method of alignment used.

In some cases, only one hub is secured, usually the stationary machine, and the other is pulled back on the shaft so the coupling face can be measured.

Objective 14   Describe the Operation of the Straight Edge and Feeler Gauge Alignment Method

Straight Edge and Feeler Gauge Alignment Method Steps

The general procedure just described is used by the straight edge and feeler gauge method to align two shafts. These are the specific steps to follow:

- Perform Pre-Alignment Steps
- Perform Vertical Angular Alignment
- Perform Vertical Parallel Alignment
- Perform Horizontal Angular Alignment and Set Coupling Gap
- Perform Horizontal Parallel Alignment

Perform Pre-Alignment Steps

Before starting the alignment process, perform these pre-alignment steps:

- Perform a lockout/tagout.
- Clean and make free of burrs the motor and driven machine's baseplate, shims, and mounting surface.
- Mount the motor and driven machine and tighten bolts.
- Check both machines for an initial soft foot.
- Check both machines for a final soft foot.
- Check both shafts for run-out and end float.
- Level both shafts.
- Make sure the height of the stationary machine is higher than the machine to be moved (MTBM).
- Clean the coupling of dirt or grease and mount the coupling hubs on the shafts.
- Adjust the positions of the two machines so that the gap between the couplings halves is approximately the amount recommended by the manufacturer.
- Tighten the mounting bolts of the two machines.

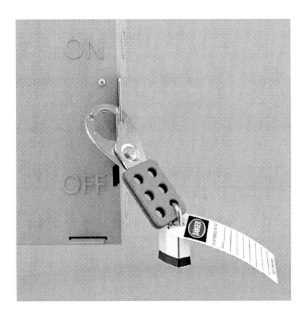

Perform Vertical Angular Alignment

First, mark the two coupling halves with a chalk or ink mark at a place on the hubs that is free of nicks or burrs. This is where you will take all of your measurements during the alignment process.

Next, rotate the coupling hubs so that the two chalk marks are both at the 0° position. Use a feeler gauge to measure the gap between the two coupling hubs at 0°. Select the feeler gauge leaf or leaves that will give a slight drag when passed through the gap.

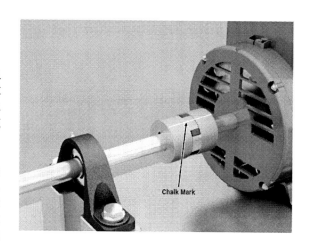

Chalk Mark

Make sure you do not insert the feeler gauge leaves more than 1/2 inch. With angular alignment, your measurement will vary depending on how far you stick in the leaves. Next, rotate the coupling hubs so that the chalk marks are at the 180° position and measure the gap here. The difference between the two measurements is the amount of vertical angular misalignment.

For example, if the top gap is 0.010 inch and the bottom gap is 0.017 inch, the misalignment is 0.007 inch. To correct this misalignment, shim the front two feet or the back two.

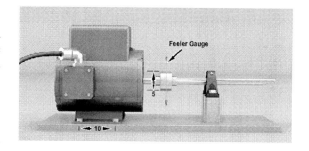

Feeler Gauge

You can determine the amount of shims needed by multiplying the misalignment by the shim ratio. The shim ratio is the ratio of the mounting bolt distance to the hub diameter. For example, the shim ratio shown here is 2 (10 ÷ 5). The amount to shim then is 0.014 (2 × 0.007).

If the gap is larger at the top, shim the back two feet. If it is larger at the bottom, shim the front two feet.

The reason you are rotating the coupling hubs before making each measurement is so that you can take measurements off of the same places on the hubs each time. This avoids errors in measurement caused by imperfections on the outside diameters (rims) of the coupling hubs.

In some cases, one or both of the shafts will not rotate by hand. You can still use this procedure, but you will not be as accurate.

Perform Vertical Parallel Alignment

Before checking the vertical alignment, or offset, first, measure the hub diameters to determine if the hubs are the same size. When hubs have different diameters, the alignment steps are different.

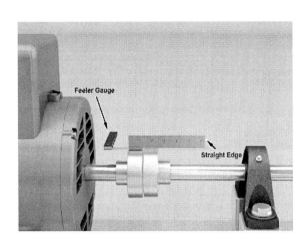

If they are the same size, rotate the two marks to the 0° position and measure the offset. Do this by placing a straight edge on the hub that is higher and measuring the gap with a feeler gauge, as shown here.

Next, rotate the coupling hubs so that the chalk marks are at the 180° position and measure the gap here. If the two measurements are the same, this is the amount of vertical parallel misalignment, or offset.

If they are different, calculate the average of the two and use this as the vertical offset. Shim all four motor feet equally with shims having the same thickness as the offset you measured.

If the diameters of the two hubs are different, shim the MTBM so that the hub gap is the same on both sides, as shown here.

Perform Horizontal Angular Alignment and Set Coupling Gap

First, center the end-play of the driver shaft and the driven shaft if they have any. Then rotate the chalk marks to the 90° position and use either a steel rule or feeler gauge to measure the gap, as shown here.

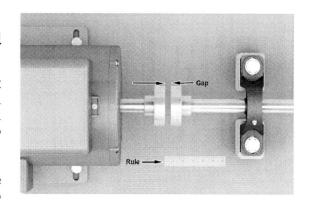

Loosen the mounting bolts and move the MTBM either in or out to adjust the gap to the manufacturer's specifications. This amount will vary, depending on the type of coupling.

Now rotate the marks to the 270° position and measure the gap again. Adjust the position of the motor so that the gap is the same on both sides at both 90° and 270° and is within the manufacturer's gap specification.

Perform Horizontal Parallel Alignment

Use a straight edge and feeler gauge to measure the misalignment when the chalk marks are at the 90° and 270° positions, as shown here.

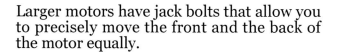

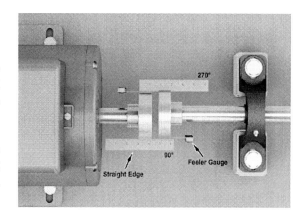

Carefully bump or move the side of the motor without losing angular alignment until the offset measurements at 90° and 270° are the same or zero.

Larger motors have jack bolts that allow you to precisely move the front and the back of the motor equally.

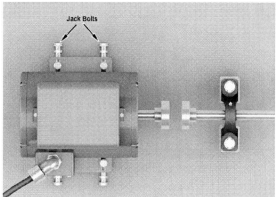

Recheck the gap and horizontal alignments until the settings are within the manufacturer's specifications. Next tighten down the motor's mounting bolts. Then recheck all measurements.

If any one of the five measurements is outside its allowable tolerance, repeat the alignment procedure.

Module 4 Introduction to V-Belt Drives

Segment 1   Belt Drive Concepts

Objective 1   Describe the Function of the Three Basic Components of a Belt Drive

Belt Drive Components

A belt drive consists of three basic components:

• Belt
• Driver Sheave
• Driven Sheave

Belt

The belt is a continuous loop of material, usually made mostly of rubber with some other materials.

The belt is stretched between the two sheaves and transmits speed and torque by means of the friction between it and the sheave grooves.

Driver Sheave

The driver sheave, also called a pulley, is a grooved disc that is attached to the shaft of the drive or prime mover. It turns with the drive shaft and causes the belt to move.

Driven Sheave

The driven sheave, a pulley, is a grooved disc that is attached to the driven shaft. It turns when the belt moves, which causes the driven shaft to rotate.

Belt Drive Speed and Torque

The relative diameters of the driven sheave and the driver sheave determine the speed and torque which are transmitted to the driven shaft.

The ratio of the sizes of the sheaves can be selected to either decrease or increase the speed and the torque delivered to the driven shaft, but if speed is increased, torque is decreased, and vice versa.

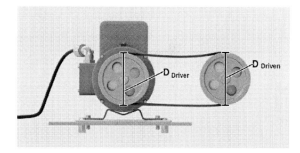

Objective 2   Define Pitch and Explain Its Importance

Pitch Definition

Calculation of the speed and torque delivered to the driven shaft by an adjacent shaft drive (either belt, chain, or gear) is based on a concept called pitch.

Pitch is defined as the distance between a point and a similar corresponding point. Examples of pitch are shown for screw threads, chains, and gears.

Although the V-belt itself does not have an associated pitch, the belt drive does have three pitch-derived features which are used to calculate speed and torque: pitch diameter, pitch circle, and pitch length.

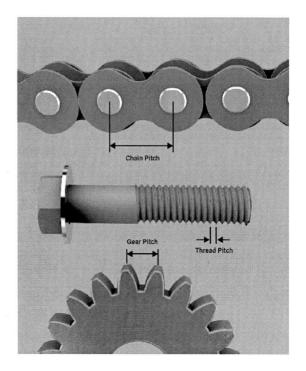

Objective 3 Define the Pitch Circle, Pitch Diameter and Pitch Length of a Belt Drive and Explain Their Importance

Two Disc Transmission

Pitch circle, pitch diameter, and pitch length are based on the concept that speed and torque can be transmitted from one shaft to another shaft.

Imagining the surfaces of two discs in contact with each other, the friction between the discs will cause the driver disc to make the driven disc turn.

Assuming that the discs have no slip between them, the surface speeds of the contacting edges of the discs are the same.

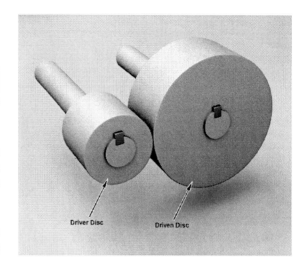

Driver Disc   Driven Disc

Two Disc Transmission Operation

In order for the driver disc to turn the driven disc, the drive motor must create a torque causing a force where the two discs contact each other.

This force creates a torque in the driven disc and is the same on both discs at the point where they contact each other.

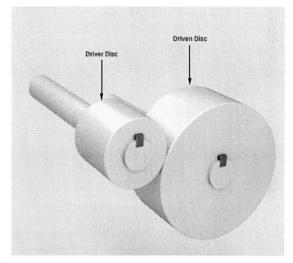

Driver Disc   Driven Disc

Belt Drive Transmission

The belt drive also transmits speed and torque using the same concepts, except that the two discs are separated.

The belt acts as an extension which contacts the two discs, therefore you can treat them as if they were in contact with each other.

Pitch Circle of a Disc Drive System

The pitch circle is defined as the circle that goes through the place on each disc where the speed and force are transmitted.

In the case of the two discs, the pitch circle represents the outer surface of each disc.

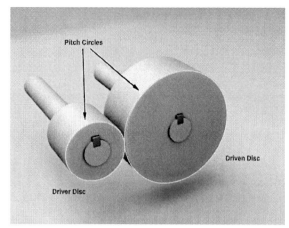

Pitch Circle of a Belt Drive System

The pitch circle of the belt drive is not the outer edge of the hub, but is the place in the belt representing the center of the force being transmitted through the belt.

In the case of a V-belt, the pitch circle is located somewhere inside the outer diameter of the sheave.

The pitch circle is important only because it allows you to determine the pitch diameter.

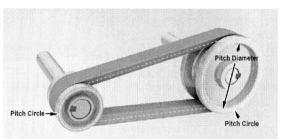

Pitch Diameter

The pitch diameter is simply the diameter of the pitch circle.

This is important because it allows calculation of the speed and torque being transmitted to the driven shaft.

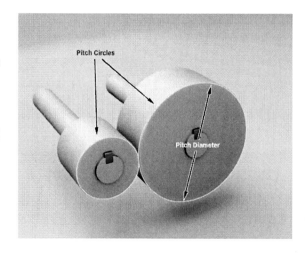

Pitch Length

Pitch length is the length of the belt that passes through the pitch circles of the two sheaves.

The pitch length is important because it is used to size the belt.

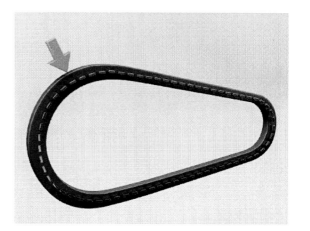

Objective 4   Describe How to Calculate the Pulley Ratio and Explain Its Importance

Pulley Ratio Description

One of the reasons to use a belt drive is to make the speed or the torque of the driven shaft different than that of the driver shaft.

This is accomplished by making the relative sizes of the sheaves or pulleys different.

The ratio of the pitch diameters of the two sheaves is called the pulley ratio and is used to directly calculate the speed and torque of the driven shaft, given the driver shaft speed and torque.

Pulley Ratio

$$PR = \frac{D_{DVN}}{D_{DVR}}$$

Where:

D_{DVR} = Pitch Diameter of Driver Pulley (inches)

D_{DVN} = Pitch Diameter of Driven Pulley (inches)

PR = Pulley Ratio

Pulley Ratio Example

As an example, look at the belt drive system shown. The pitch diameters of the driver and driven pulleys are 2 inches and 6 inches respectively.

This means that the pulley ratio is 6/2, or 3. This is often stated as a 3:1 pulley ratio.

It is important to remember that the pulley ratio is determined using the pitch diameter, which is not the same as the outer diameter of a pulley. If you use the outer diameter, your answer will have a slight error.

Effect of Pulley Ratio on Shaft Speed

To understand why the pulley ratio affects shaft speed, look at case A.

In this example, the circumferences of the two discs turn the same amount because the contacting discs are the same size.

If, however, the discs are not the same size, as shown in case B, the circumferences will still turn by the same amount but the number of revolutions will be different.

In case B, the driven disc is two times the diameter of the driver disc meaning that its circumference is also two times as large.

Therefore, for each turn of the driver disc, the driven disc rotates the circumference of the driver disc, which is one half the circumference of the driven disc.

This means that the driven disc only rotates one half turn.

Case A

Case B

Effect of Pulley Ratio on Belt Drive Speed

The same relationship also applies to belt drives. As the outer edge of the drive pulley rotates, the belt transfers an equal amount of movement to the outer edge of the driven pulley.

If the pulleys are of different sizes, the driven shaft rotation speed will be different than the driver shaft rotation speed.

As shown, the larger pulley decreases the speed delivered to the driven shaft.

Effect of Pulley Ratio on Torque

In a similar manner to speed, the pulley ratio also affects the torque transmitted to the driven shaft. To understand why, you should recall that the force applied to the surfaces of the two pulleys is the same.

Since the torque radius is the radius of the pulley, the torque in one pulley will be different than another if its radius (or diameter) is different.

This is a common sense concept that you can use on the job to determine in general how power is being changed by the mechanical drive system.

Effects on Torque

In the case of the example shown, the torque in the driver pulley is 5 in.-lbs (Driver Torque=5×1=5).

The torque in the driven pulley, however, is 15 in.-lbs (Driven Torque=5×3=15). The larger pulley increased the torque delivered to the driven shaft.

In other words, the larger pulley turns more slowly but has greater torque.

Driven Torque = 15 in.-lbs
Driven Diameter = 6 in.

Driver Torque = 5 in.-lbs
Driver Diameter = 2 in.

Objective 5   Describe How to Calculate the Shaft Speed and Torque of a Belt Drive System

Belt Drive Speed

The relationship between pulley sizes and shaft speeds of a belt drive can be expressed in the formula shown.

The top formula reveals that the shaft speeds are inversely proportional to the pitch diameters. This means that an increase in pulley size causes the speed to decrease.

Notice that the right hand side of the top formula is the pulley ratio, so the formula can also be stated as shown in the bottom formula.

Belt Drive Speed

$$\frac{S_{DVR}}{S_{DVN}} = \frac{D_{DVN}}{D_{DVR}}$$

Where:

S_{DVR} = Driver Rotational Speed (rpm)

S_{DVN} = Driven Rotational Speed (rpm)

D_{DVN} = Driven Pitch Diameter (ft or m)

D_{DVR} = Driver Pitch Diameter (ft or m)

Belt Drive Speed

$$\frac{S_{DVR}}{S_{DVN}} = PR$$

Where:

S_{DVR} = Driver Rotational Speed (rpm)

S_{DVN} = Driven Rotational Speed (rpm)

PR = Pulley Ratio

Belt Drive Torque

The shaft torque formula shown on top is similar to the shaft speed formula, except that the torque is directly, not inversely, proportional to the pitch diameters.

As with the shaft speed formula, the torque formula shown on top can be modified to use the pulley ratio.

Belt Drive Torque

$$\frac{T_{DVN}}{T_{DVR}} = \frac{D_{DVN}}{D_{DVR}}$$

Where:

T_{DVN} = Driven Rotational Torque (ft-lbs or N-m)

T_{DVR} = Driver Rotational Torque (ft-lbs or N-m)

D_{DVN} = Driven Pitch Diameter (ft or m)

D_{DVR} = Driver Pitch Diameter (ft or m)

Belt Drive Torque

$$\frac{T_{DVN}}{T_{DVR}} = PR$$

Where:

T_{DVN} = Driven Rotational Torque (ft-lbs or N-m)

T_{DVR} = Driver Rotational Torque (ft-lbs or N-m)

PR = Pulley Ratio

Mechanical Power Relation

It is important to note that torque and speed changes transmitted to the driven shaft are actually related to each other by way of the mechanical power.

The power that is transferred between the driver shaft and the driver sheave is the same as the power transferred between the driven sheave and the driven shaft, apart from minor losses.

Since power is equal to speed times torque, any change in speed caused by a pulley ratio must carry with it an equal and opposite change in torque. Otherwise, the law of conservation of energy would be broken.

Segment 2   V-Belt Operation

Objective 6   List Five Types of Belt Drives and Give an Application of Each

Belt Drive Types

Belt drives are the most common type of adjacent or parallel shaft-to-shaft drives used because they are quiet, low in cost, and easy to maintain.

These are the five types of belt drives you will most often encounter:

- Flat Belt
- V-Belt
- Timing Belt
- Round Belt
- Ribbed Belt

Flat Belt

The flat belt was the first type of belt drive used.

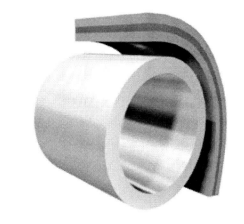

It originated during the industrial revolution of the 19th century when factories transmitted power to individual machines with long rotating shafts running the length of the factory.

The power from these shafts was transmitted to each machine by means of two pulleys and a flat belt.

Today, flat belts are rarely used to drive machines because they are not very efficient, they are bulky, they are not well suited to higher motor speeds, and they require more maintenance than other types of belt drives.

However, flat belts are still commonly used as conveyors.

V-Belt

The V-belt is a wedge-shaped belt made from a combination of rubber and textile material.

The V-belt is designed to grip the walls of a grooved pulley by wedging itself against the sides of the pulley groove as the belt is tightened.

These are the advantages of the V-belt over the flat belt:

- It can operate at higher speeds.
- It can transmit power more efficiently.
- It can transmit power in a smaller size.
- It requires very little maintenance.

The V-belt drive is commonly used in applications such as fan drives, air compressors, and car engines.

Timing Belt

One of the general problems of V-belts is they can slip during operation. The timing belt solves this problem by using a belt and pulleys which have notches or teeth.

As the drive pulley turns, its teeth engage the teeth of the belt and pull it. With this design, the belt does not slip, and a constant speed is maintained at the shaft.

Because of the teeth, the timing belt does not require a high tension as V-belts do, making its operation more efficient.

The timing belt is used in some car engines to maintain a constant speed between devices that must operate together.

It is also used in positioning applications, such as the axes of robots and electronic circuit board assembly machines, to accurately move to various positions.

Timing belts are also called positive drive belts, synchronous drive belts, and gear belts.

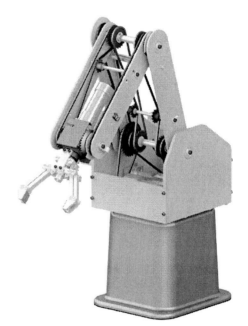

Round Belt

The round belt uses a circular cross-section.

It is mainly found in very light duty applications, such as vacuums and printers, where either the load is light or slip and efficiency are not important. Its main asset is low cost.

Ribbed Belt

The ribbed belt has ribs that run longitudinally (along the length) on the belt. These ribs are designed to seat in mating grooves in the sheaves.

This type of belt has a greater area of the belt in contact with the sheave, which means that there is less wear on the belt or sheaves.

The sheaves are more compact and higher pulley ratios can be used, typically as high as 40:1.

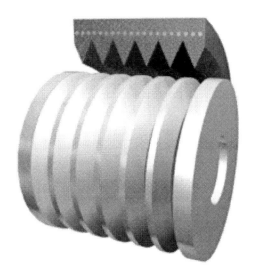

Objective 7   List Three Types of V-Belts and Give an Application of Each

Three V-Belt Types

There are three main types of V-belts:

- Fractional Horsepower V-Belt
- Conventional V-Belt
- Wedge V-Belt

Each type of belt is designed for a particular type of power range and duty cycle.

These belts look similar, differing mainly in dimensions and internal construction.

Fractional Horsepower V-Belt

The fractional horsepower (FHP) V-belt, also called a light duty belt, is designed for low-power intermittent applications, below 7.5 hp. A typical application is a small air compressor or a fan.

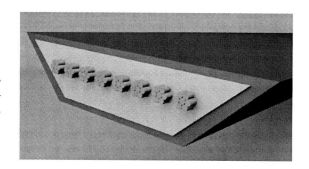

Conventional V-Belt

The conventional V-belt, also called a standard multiple or standard duty V-belt, is designed for continuous duty applications up to 300 hp.

They can be used singly, but are often used in sets of more than one belt, which is where the term multiple comes from.

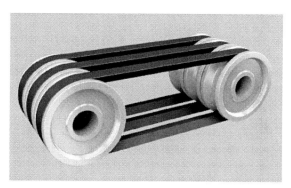

The conventional V-belt is the type of belt you will find most often in industrial applications. It is used for many items, including large air compressors and fans.

Wedge V-Belt

In 1958, a new family of V-belts called wedge V-belts, also called heavy duty or narrow-series V-belts, was jointly developed by the Gates Rubber Company and the Dodge Company.

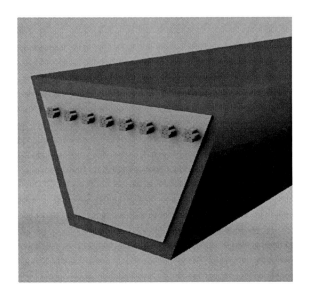

This belt improved the power-carrying capability of the V-belt for a given cross section size, allowing smaller sheaves to be used.

The wedge belt is designed for continuous duty service and can be used at power levels up to 500 hp and in either single or multiple sets.

The wedge belt is used in industrial applications where either heavy duty shock loads might occur, there is a need for a smaller size, or if the load is higher than what can be handled by a conventional belt.

Objective 8   Describe the Operation of a Fractional Horsepower V-Belt Drive

V-Belt Drive Functioning

V-belt drives transmit power by increasing the distance between the two sheaves so that tension is created on the belt.

This tension causes the belt to be pulled down, or wedged, into the groove of the sheave, creating enough friction to keep the belt from slipping when the turning sheave is placed under a load.

It is important to note that the wedging action of the V-belt creates friction between the sides of the sheave, not the groove bottom.

The V-belt should ride high in the groove, with its top near the top of the sheave. Normally, the V-belt does not touch the bottom of the sheave.

FHP V-Belts

The belt used in a fractional horsepower (FHP) V-belt drive consists of polyester or some other textile-based cording, rubber filler compound, and a neoprene envelope.

This neoprene envelope makes the outside of the belt smooth.

Because the FHP belts are made for light duty service, they are usually smaller; the cords are weaker and less numerous than in the conventional and wedge belts.

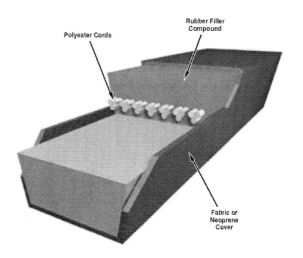

FHP Sheaves

The sheaves used for FHP drives are usually made of either stamped steel halves which are pressed together, die cast zinc, or die cast aluminum.

The sheaves are normally attached to the shafts with an integral hub which has the keyseat built into the sheave. This is called a finished bore or fixed bore hub.

FHP V-Belt Sizing

The FHP belt sizes are designated by a number and an L in the part number while conventional belts are designated by just a letter (A, B, C, D, etc.).

It is important to know that two L belts, the 4L and 5L, are the same size as two conventional belts, the A and B, respectively.

As a result, most manufacturers are phasing out the 4L and 5L belts and using the A and B belts with FHP sheaves of those sizes.

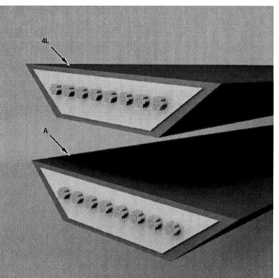

Objective 9   Describe How to Install and Align a V-Belt Drive

Installing and Aligning a V-Belt

V-belt drives are easy to install, but it is important to do it correctly in order for the belts to last as long as possible.

Regardless of the type of V-belt you are using, the installation steps are similar.

- Step 1. Mount and Level
- Step 2. Inspect the Sheaves
- Step 3. Mount the Sheaves onto the Shafts
- Step 4. Mount the Belt
- Step 5. Align the Sheaves
- Step 6. Apply Initial Tension to the Belt
- Step 7. Run the Motor Briefly to Seat the Belts
- Step 8. Stop the Motor and Re-Tension the Belt
- Step 9. Re-Tension the Belt

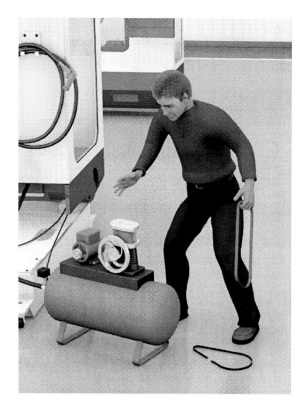

Step 1. Mount and Level

Leveling the shafts is actually part of the alignment of the sheaves, which is step 5 of this process.

However, it is easier to place a level on the shaft before the sheaves are attached.

As a part of this process, the motor and driven component should also be checked for a soft foot and excessive run-out.

Step 2. Inspect the Sheaves

If the sheaves have nicks, burrs, or gouges, replace them, as this can cause the belt to be cut.

If a sheave is found to be excessively worn when checked with a sheave gauge, replace it.

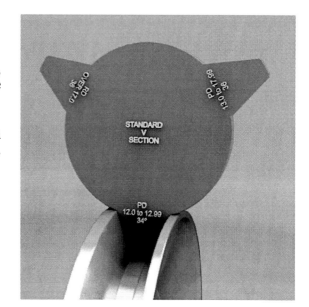

Also, make sure that the sheaves do not have any dirt, oil, grease, or rust on them.

Dirt and rust can cause the belt to wear quickly. Oil and grease can attack the belt material and destroy it.

Use a stiff brush to remove dirt and rust. Wipe clean all oil and grease.

Step 3. Mount the Sheaves onto the Shafts

The sheaves should be attached to the shafts using either a finished bore hub or a bushing.

Bushings are commonly used on industrial V-belt drives that use conventional or wedge belts.

After you install the sheaves, make sure that the sheaves do not wobble by rotating the shafts and observing their motion. If they wobble, reinstall them or use other sheaves.

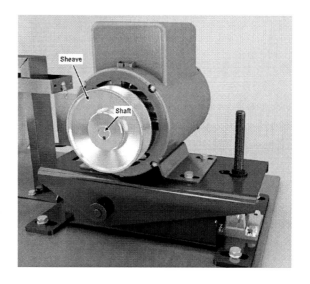

Step 4. Mount the Belt

To mount the belt, first loosen the mounting bolts of the motor and slide it toward the driven shaft.

This will reduce the center distance between the two sheaves so that the belt can be slipped loosely over the sheaves without forcing it.

Next, place the belt over the sheaves.

The belt should never be forced onto the sheaves.

Doing this will damage the belt, either by creating a nick in the belt or by breaking or weakening the internal fibers. In either case, this can severely shorten the life of the belt.

Also, the belt should never be run on, which is placing the belt over the sheaves while the sheaves are rotating, as this has the same effect as forcing the belt onto the sheaves.

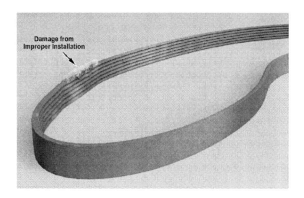

Step 5. Align the Sheaves

Just as with couplings, it is important to align sheaves since misaligned sheaves will cause the belt and the bearings to wear quickly.

This misalignment can appear in several ways. The goal of alignment is to avoid twisting the belt.

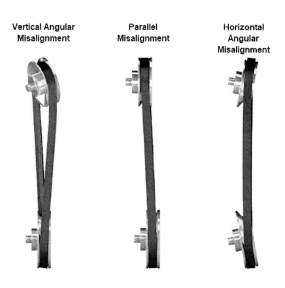

Step 6. Apply Initial Tension to the Belt

The proper belt tension is very important to the life of the drive as some tension is necessary for the belt to grip the sheave.

If the tension is too high, the bearings and the belt will also wear quickly.

If the tension is too little, however, the belt will slip, causing the belt and the sheaves to wear quickly.

Tensioning the belt is a 3-step process:

• Determine the tension needed
• Apply tension to the belt
• Measure the tension

The belt should be tightened to approximately the correct amount as determined by several methods, but does not need to be precise at this point because the belt will stretch after it has been run.

Step 7. Run the Motor Briefly to Seat the Belts

A new belt will quickly stretch and be forced lower into the grooves when it runs under a load.

Both of these actions cause the tension to decrease.

Step 8. Stop the Motor and Re-Tension the Belt

After about one minute, stop the drive and check the tension again.

Adjust the tension so that it is within the acceptable range.

Step 9. Re-Tension the Belt

During the first few days of operation, the belt will stretch enough that it should be re-tensioned again.

Two Methods Used to Align the Sheaves

Sheave alignment can be done in one of two ways:

• With a Level
• With a String

With a Level

The sheaves can be aligned by first leveling the two shafts using a spirit level. A straight edge is placed against the faces of the sheaves to align the sheave grooves, and the parallelism of the shafts is checked. If this has already been done as part of mounting the motor, this step can be skipped.

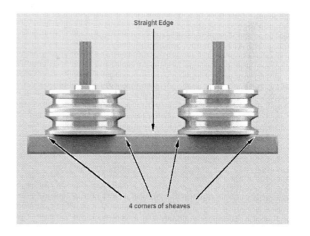

The faces of the sheaves should be made so that they are flush against the straight edge. When this occurs, the shafts are parallel and the sheave grooves are aligned.

The faces of the sheaves are aligned when four corners are in contact with the straight edge.

With a String

If you do not have a straight edge, or the distance between sheave centers is too great, you can use a string.

First attach one end of the string to the shaft of the driven sheave, then pull the string taut and straight so that it touches both edges of the driven sheave.

If the drive sheave's edges do not touch, the sheaves are misaligned. Adjust the position of the drive shaft so that the edges of the drive sheave also touch the string.

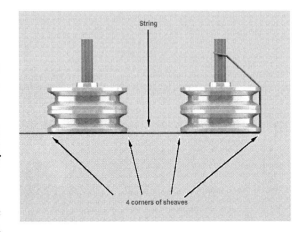

Segment 3   Belt Tensioning

Objective 10   Describe How to Determine Belt Tension for an Application

Belt Deflection Force

The first step to perform in order to tension a belt drive is to determine how much tension to apply to it.

Belt tension is measured by how much force is needed to deflect the belt a certain distance.

This is called the belt deflection force, and the method that is used to measure belt tension in this way is called the belt deflection method.

Allowable Belt Deflection Force

The amount of belt deflection force is found in tables.

This table is available from belt suppliers and shows the specific force for each belt, according to the belt's size, sheave size, operating speed, and whether it is new or old.

Cross Section	Sheave Diameter		Minimum Deflection Force - LBS			
	Smallest Sheave Diameter Range	RPM Range	Belt Deflection Force			
			Unnotched Belts		Notched Belts	
			Used Belt	New Belt	Used Belt	New Belt
A, AX	2.0 - 3.0	1000 - 2500	2.8	4.3	3.8	4.8
		2501 - 4000	2.0	3.3	3.1	3.9
	3.0 - 3.6	1000 - 2500	3.7	5.5	4.1	6.1
		2501 - 4000	2.8	4.2	3.4	5.0
	3.8 - 4.8	1000 - 2500	4.5	6.8	5.0	7.4
		2501 - 4000	3.8	5.7	4.3	6.4
	5.0 - 7.0	1000 - 2500	5.4	8.0	5.7	9.4
		2501 - 4000	4.7	7.0	5.1	7.6
B, BX	3.4 - 4.2	860 - 2500			4.9	7.2
		2501 - 4000			4.2	6.2
	4.4 - 5.6	860 - 2500	5.3	7.9	7.1	10.5
		2501 - 4000	4.5	6.7	7.1	9.1
	5.8 - 8.6	860 - 2500	6.3	9.4	8.5	12.6
		2501 - 4000	6.0	8.9	7.3	10.9
C, CX	7.0 - 9.0	500 - 1740	11.5	17.0	14.7	21.8
		1741 -3000	9.4	13.8	11.9	17.5
	9.5 - 16.0	500 - 1740	14.1	21.0	15.9	23.5
		1741 -3000	12.5	18.5	14.6	21.6

Force Limits

The force levels listed in the table refer to the minimum level of tension force.

The upper limit of the acceptable tension force is 50% greater than the lower limit.

Therefore, the tension of the belt should be between the force level listed in the table and 1.5 times that value.

The ideal tension is the lower of the two values.

It represents the least tension needed to transmit the force and allow no slipping.

If the tension is greater, more energy is lost through friction.

Cross Section	Sheave Diameter		Minimum Deflection Force - LBS			
	Smallest Sheave Diameter Range	RPM Range	Belt Deflection Force			
			Unnotched Belts		Notched Belts	
			Used Belt	New Belt	Used Belt	New Belt
A, AX	2.0 - 3.0	1000 - 2500	2.8	4.3	3.8	4.8
		2501 - 4000	2.0	3.3	3.1	3.9
	3.0 - 3.6	1000 - 2500	3.7	5.5	4.1	6.1
		2501 - 4000	2.8	4.2	3.4	5.0
	3.8 - 4.8	1000 - 2500	4.5	6.8	5.0	7.4
		2501 - 4000	3.8	5.7	4.3	6.4
	5.0 - 7.0	1000 - 2500	5.4	8.0	5.7	9.4
		2501 - 4000	4.7	7.0	5.1	7.6
B, BX	3.4 - 4.2	860 - 2500			4.9	7.2
		2501 - 4000			4.2	6.2
	4.4 - 5.6	860 - 2500	5.3	7.9	7.1	10.5
		2501 - 4000	4.5	6.7	7.1	9.1
	5.8 - 8.6	860 - 2500	6.3	9.4	8.5	12.6
		2501 - 4000	6.0	8.9	7.3	10.9
C, CX	7.0 - 9.0	500 - 1740	11.5	17.0	14.7	21.8
		1741 -3000	9.4	13.8	11.9	17.5
	9.5 - 16.0	500 - 1740	14.1	21.0	15.9	23.5
		1741 -3000	12.5	18.5	14.6	21.6

Lower Limit = 2.0
Upper Limit = 2.0 x 1.5 = 3.0

Objective 11   Describe Three Methods of Adjusting Belt Tension

Belt Tensioning Methods

Tension is applied to the belt by moving the driver motor away from the driven shaft.

This can be done with either a pry bar, punch, or adjustable mounting base.

While moving the motor, make sure to maintain sheave alignment by holding the straight edge against the sheaves, or at least rechecking the alignment after tensioning.

Segment 4 Belt Tension Measurement

Objective 12 Describe Three Methods of Measuring Belt Tension and Give an Application of Each

Tension Measurement Methods

Once the belt tension has been initially set, the next step is to measure the tension to make sure that it is correct.

There are three ways that belt tension can be measured:

• Hand Pressure
• Tension Tester
• Spring Scale and Straight Edge

Hand Pressure

The most basic way to test the tension is to use the sense of touch.

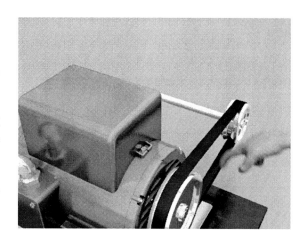

To do this, strike the belt with your hand. It will feel alive and springy when it is tensioned correctly.

If the tension is too low, the belt will feel dead. Too much tension will make it feel taut, with no give at all.

Both fractional horsepower and conventional belts can be tested this way.

Wedge belts cannot because the tension they require is too high. They require a tension tester.

Tension Tester

A more accurate method of tension measurement is the force deflection method, using a tension tester or belt tension checker.

The tension tester is a handheld device which measures belt tension by measuring the force needed to deflect the belt a certain amount.

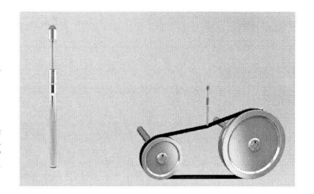

To perform the test, the tester should be placed in the middle of the belt span and forced down until the belt is deflected by the proper amount.

The force indicated by the tension tester is then read and compared to a recommended force deflection range for that particular belt. This is available in a table like the one shown.

The amount of tension tester deflection depends on how far apart the centers of the sheaves are (the size of the belt span) and should be 1/64 of the belt span. The belt span is the distance between the points on the sheaves where the belt touches each sheave.

The force should be at least as high as the recommended force level but no higher than 50% above it.

Cross Section	Sheave Diameter		Minimum Deflection Force - LBS			
			Belt Deflection Force			
	Smallest Sheave Diameter Range	RPM Range	Unnotched Belts		Notched Belts	
			Used Belt	New Belt	Used Belt	New Belt
A, AX	2.0 - 3.0	1000 - 2500	2.8	4.3	3.8	4.8
		2501 - 4000	2.0	3.3	3.1	3.9
	3.0 - 3.6	1000 - 2500	3.7	5.5	4.1	6.1
		2501 - 4000	2.8	4.2	3.4	5.0
	3.8 - 4.8	1000 - 2500	4.5	6.8	5.0	7.4
		2501 - 4000	3.8	5.7	4.3	6.4
	5.0 - 7.0	1000 - 2500	5.4	8.0	5.7	9.4
		2501 - 4000	4.7	7.0	5.1	7.6
B, BX	3.4 - 4.2	860 - 2500			4.9	7.2
		2501 - 4000			4.2	6.2
	4.4 - 5.6	860 - 2500	5.3	7.9	7.1	10.5
		2501 - 4000	4.5	6.7	7.1	9.1
	5.8 - 8.6	860 - 2500	6.3	9.4	8.5	12.6
		2501 - 4000	6.0	8.9	7.3	10.9
C, CX	7.0 - 9.0	500 - 1740	11.5	17.0	14.7	21.8
		1741 -3000	9.4	13.8	11.9	17.5
	9.5 - 16.0	500 - 1740	14.1	21.0	15.9	23.5
		1741 -3000	12.5	18.5	14.6	21.6

If the belt speed exceeds the speed listed in the table, the tension should be reduced as recommended by the manufacturer.

The tension tester is the preferred method for checking belt tension for any type of belt. Proper tension will lead to a longer life of the mechanical components in the system.

Spring Scale and Straight Edge

The spring scale and straight edge method is similar to the tension tester in that it is a type of force deflection method. With this method, the spring scale is used to deflect the belt.

The amount of deflection is determined in the same way as described with the tension tester, 1/64 of the belt span.

This is measured by placing a straight edge across the belt span and measuring with a ruler.

Module 5 Introduction to Chain Drives

Segment 1   Chain Drive Concepts

Objective 1   Describe the Function of the Three Basic Components of a Chain Drive

Three Components of a Chain Drive

A chain drive consists of three basic components:

- Chain
- Driver Sprocket
- Driven Sprocket

Chain

The chain is a continuous loop of links, usually having steel rollers, wrapped around two toothed wheels called sprockets.

The chain transmits speed and torque between the two sprockets.

Driver Sprocket

A sprocket is a disc-shaped component with teeth that is mounted to a shaft. Sprockets are normally made of strong, high carbon steel. They can be attached to shafts using an integral hub with a keyseat or with a bushing.

The driver sprocket is mounted to the shaft of the driver or prime mover. When the driver shaft turns, the driver sprocket turns, applying its speed and torque to the chain and causing it to move.

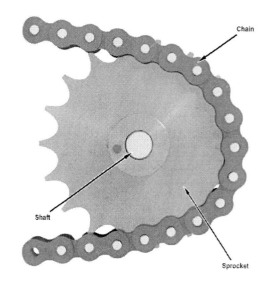

Driven Sprocket

The driven sprocket is mounted to the driven shaft. It turns when the chain moves, which causes the driven shaft to rotate.

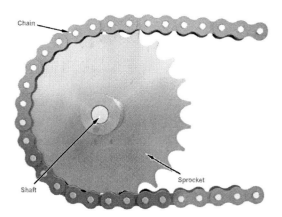

Gear Teeth Ratio Effects

The relative number of teeth between the driven sprocket and the driver sprocket determines the speed and torque of the driven shaft. The ratio of the teeth of the two sprockets can be selected to either increase or decrease either the speed or the torque delivered to the driven shaft.

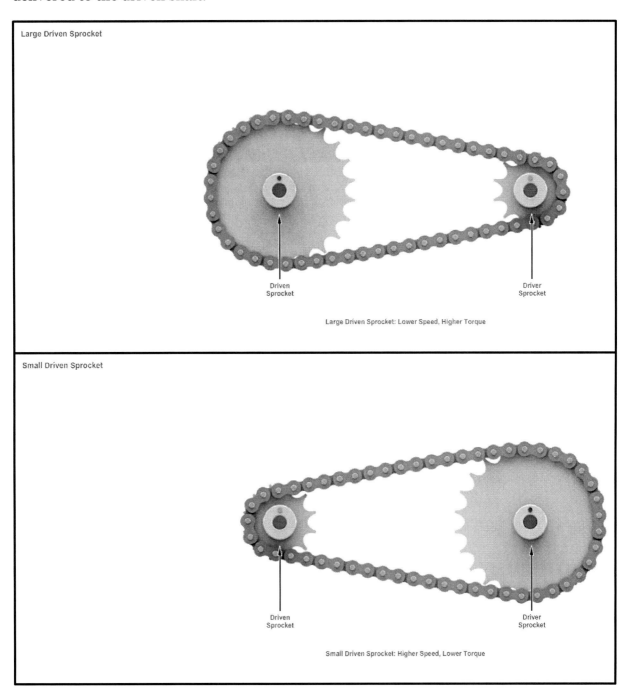

Large Driven Sprocket

Driven Sprocket

Driver Sprocket

Large Driven Sprocket: Lower Speed, Higher Torque

Small Driven Sprocket

Driven Sprocket

Driver Sprocket

Small Driven Sprocket: Higher Speed, Lower Torque

Objective 2   Describe How to Calculate Sprocket Ratio and Explain Its Importance

Calculating Sprocket Ratio

The speed and torque that are transmitted to the driven shaft of a chain drive can be calculated by using the sprocket ratio.

The sprocket ratio is the ratio of the number of teeth on the driven sprocket to the number of teeth on the driver sprocket.

In the example shown the sprocket ratio is calculated to be 3.

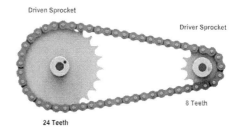

Driven Sprocket

Driver Sprocket

8 Teeth

24 Teeth

Sprocket Ratio Formula

$$R = \frac{N_{DVN}}{N_{DRV}}$$

Where:

R = Sprocket Ratio

N_{DVN} = Number of Teeth on Driven Sprocket

N_{DRV} = Number of Teeth on Driver Sprocket

Insert Known Values:

$N_{DVN} = 24$

$N_{DRV} = 8$

$$R = \frac{N_{DVN}}{N_{DRV}}$$

Calculate Result:

$$R = \frac{24}{8}$$

$$R = 3$$

Chordal Action

Although it might seem that you could simply use the sprockets' pitch diameters to determine the sprocket ratio, this is not totally accurate.

The chain does not ride completely along the pitch line because each link is a rigid bar that cannot bend to follow the circular path. Instead, the chain links remain straight lines as they move around the pitch circle in a process called chordal action.

Chordal action is very similar to the motion a train makes as its straight cars move through a turn in the tracks.

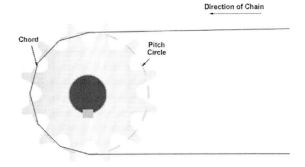

Objective 3   Describe How to Calculate Shaft Speed and Torque of a Chain Drive System

The Relationship between Sprocket Size and Speed

The speed of the driven sprocket is determined by the sprocket ratio. This is because the rate at which the teeth of the driven sprocket engage the chain is the same as the rate at which the driver sprocket teeth disengage the chain.

If the sprockets in a chain drive system have different numbers of teeth, the driven shaft's rotational speed will be different than the driver shaft's rotational speed.

The shaft with the sprocket having more teeth will have a slower rotational speed than the shaft with the sprocket having fewer teeth.

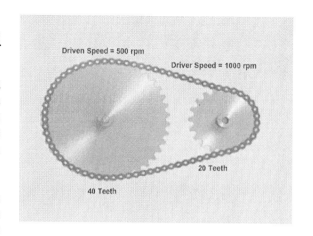

Calculating Chain Drive Speed

The relationship between numbers of sprocket teeth and shaft speeds of a chain drive can be expressed in the formula shown.

As you can see, the shaft speeds are inversely proportional to the number of teeth. This means that an increase in sprocket size, which means more teeth on the sprocket, causes the speed to decrease.

Notice that the right-hand side of the formula is the sprocket ratio so the formula can also be stated as shown.

Chain Drive Speed Formula

$$\frac{S_{DRV}}{S_{DVN}} = \frac{N_{DVN}}{N_{DRV}}$$

Where:

S_{DRV} = Driver Rotational Speed (rpm)

S_{DVN} = Driven Rotational Speed (rpm)

N_{DVN} = Number of Teeth on Driven Sprocket

N_{DRV} = Number of Teeth on Driver Sprocket

Chain Drive Speed Formula

$$\frac{S_{DRV}}{S_{DVN}} = R$$

Where:

S_{DRV} = Driver Rotational Speed (rpm)

S_{DVN} = Driven Rotational Speed (rpm)

R = Sprocket Ratio

Chain Drive Torque

The sprocket ratio also affects the torque transmitted to the driven shaft. This is because more teeth mean a larger sprocket radius and a larger sprocket radius creates more torque on the shaft.

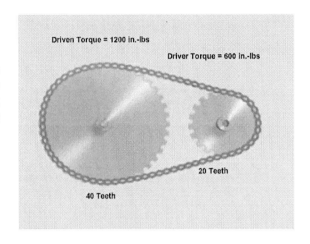

Calculating Chain Drive Torque

The formula to calculate shaft torque is similar to the shaft speed formula except that the torque is directly proportional to the number of teeth, whereas speed is inversely proportional.

As with the speed formula, the torque formula can be modified to use the sprocket ratio.

Chain Drive Torque Formula

$$\frac{T_{DVN}}{T_{DRV}} = \frac{N_{DVN}}{N_{DRV}}$$

Where:

T_{DRV} = Driver Rotational Torque (in.-lbs)

N_{DRV} = Number of Teeth on DRV Sprocket

N_{DVN} = Number of Teeth on DVN Sprocket

T_{DVN} = Driven Rotational Torque (in.-lbs)

Chain Drive Torque Formula

$$\frac{T_{DVN}}{T_{DRV}} = R$$

Where:

T_{DRV} = Driver Rotational Torque (in.-lbs)

R = Sprocket Ratio

T_{DVN} = Driven Rotational Torque (in.-lbs)

Segment 2 Chain Drive Operation

Objective 4   List Four Types of Chains and Give an Application of Each

Four Types of Chains

Chains are popular for many industrial applications. There are four common types of chains:

- Roller Chain
- Rollerless Chain
- Silent Chain
- Leaf Chain

Roller Chain

The roller chain is the most common type of chain used for mechanical drives. It has rollers mounted on pins and bushings.

These rollers roll over the teeth of the sprocket to minimize the friction and increase the efficiency of the drive.

Machinery drives, conveyor systems, robot drives, and timing drives all have roller chains.

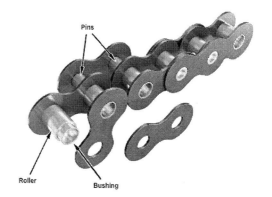

Rollerless Chain

Rollerless chains have nearly the same construction as roller chains, except they have no rollers.

Rollerless chains are used in lightweight, low-speed, mechanical drive applications where the friction between the chain and sprocket would cause little wear.

They are also used in very dirty applications that would cause roller chain bushings to wear out too quickly if the chain had rollers.

Examples include hoisting chains or drives in small cranes.

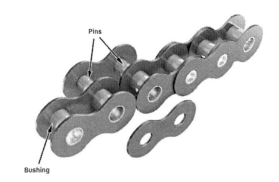

Silent Chain

The silent chain uses an inverted tooth design to reduce the noise created by the engagement and release of the sprocket teeth to the chain.

In addition to being quieter, silent chains are more efficient, last longer, and can operate at higher speeds than roller chains. However, silent chains are much more expensive than roller and rollerless chains.

Applications such as industrial pumps, fans, and other heavy machinery use silent chains.

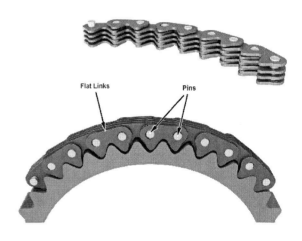

Leaf Chain

Leaf chains are made up of many plates held together by pins. They have no rollers and are not usually used in chain drive applications.

Chain wrenches, forklifts, and other hoisting devices normally use leaf chains.

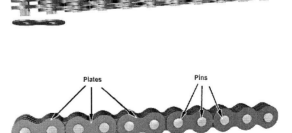

Objective 5   List Four Types of Roller Chain Drives and Give an Application of Each

Four Types of Roller Chain Drives

The roller chain is the most common type of chain used in industrial chain drive systems. There are four basic types of roller chains:

- Single-Strand Chain
- Multiple-Strand Chain
- Double-Pitch Chain
- Offset Chain

Single-Strand Chain

The single-strand chain is the most common roller chain used. A single row of rollers with plates on each side make up the chain.

Single-strand chains are used for most general-purpose applications of low-to-medium power transmissions. This type of chain is also found on bicycles.

Multiple-Strand Chain

Applications that transmit a great deal of power often use multiple-strand chains. The chains used in multiple-strand chain drives are the same as those used in single-strand drives. They are merely joined to create multiple rows.

Multiple-strand chains are used in applications with much heavier loads and higher speeds than a single-strand chain can handle.

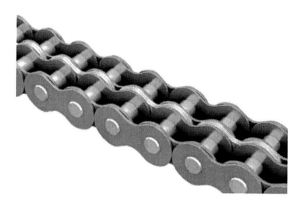

Double-Pitch Chain

Double-pitch chain has the same construction as standard roller chain except that the length of its links is twice that of the single-pitch chain.

Double-pitch chain is normally used when trying to save money on applications with low loads and speeds. They are also used in conveyor drives.

Offset Chain

Whereas standard roller chain contains two different kinds of links that mate with each other, offset chain (sometimes called cast chain) contains only one kind of link.

Because of its offset design, this type of chain doesn't require a connecting link, which is usually weaker than the rest of the chain.

For this reason, offset chain, which can be made with or without rollers, is normally made out of high strength steel to be used in heavy-load, low-speed applications.

Objective 6   Describe the Operation of a Single-Strand Roller Chain Drive

The Components of a Roller Chain

Roller chain is made up of pin links and roller links. The two types of links are alternated to form a complete link. These links mesh with the sprockets so speed and torque can be transmitted.

Pin links are made of two side plates separated by two pins.

Roller links are similar to pin links, but are made of two side plates that are separated by bushings. These bushings support the rollers that are mounted to them.

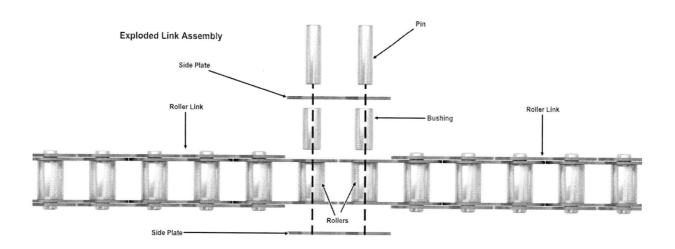

The pin of the pin link passes through the bushing on the roller link to make a complete link assembly.

The jointed link design allows the chain to flex at the junction between links. It also allows the rollers to freely roll, which reduces friction between the chain and the sprocket.

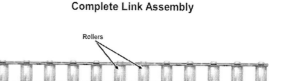

The Operation of the Roller Chain

Power is transmitted through a single-strand roller chain when the driver sprocket rotates and its teeth engage the roller links, pulling the chain around it. This causes the chain to pull on the teeth of the driven sprocket, causing it to rotate.

The chain drive does not depend on friction between the sprocket and chain to drive it. Instead, the chain drives use the engagement (or interlocking) of the sprocket teeth and chain, which creates a positive drive.

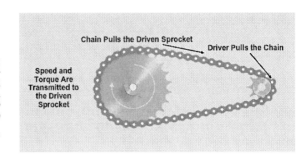

Since tooth engagement, not friction, is used to transmit the force, the chain drive does not require a high tension (as opposed to, for example, the tension in a V-belt system), which is one reason why a chain drive is more efficient than other drive systems.

The chain tension only needs to be high enough to keep the chain from flying off the sprocket during operation.

Chordal Action

The chordal action of the chain links causes some frictional losses between the sprocket and the chain. As the roller link contacts the sprocket, it initially rises up the tooth. Then, it slides down the tooth as it winds around the sprocket.

This action occurs as each link engages with the sprocket, creating a certain amount of friction. However, the friction is minimized by the chain's roller.

The rising and falling of the links also causes a slight speed variation in the chain drive. Even though the driver sprocket's speed is constant, the driven sprocket's speed oscillates.

The amount of oscillation depends on the number of teeth. If the number of teeth is greater than twenty-five, the oscillation is less than one percent and is usually disregarded.

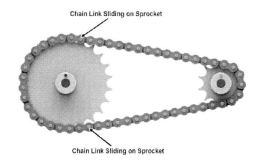

Chain Link Sliding on Sprocket

Chain Link Sliding on Sprocket

Objective 7 — Describe How to Install, Align, and Remove a Roller Chain Drive System with Adjustable Centers

Procedure for Chain Installation, Alignment, and Removal

Chain drives are easy to install, but it is important to do it correctly in order to achieve the maximum life. There are 10 steps to install, align, and remove a chain.

- Step 1. Mount and Level the Motor and the Driven Component
- Step 2. Inspect the Sprockets
- Step 3. Mount the Sprockets on the Shafts
- Step 4. Mount the Chain
- Step 5. Align the Sprockets
- Step 6. Apply Tension to the Chain
- Step 7. Apply Lubrication to the Chain
- Step 8. Run the Motor Briefly to Test the Drive
- Step 9. Recheck the Chain Sag
- Step 10. Chain Removal

Step 1. Mount and Level the Motor and the Driven Component

While leveling the shafts is actually part of aligning the sprockets, it is easier to place a level on the shaft before attaching the sprockets.

The motor and driven component should also be checked for a soft foot condition and excessive run-out. The shaft run-out should be no more than two-thousandths of an inch.

Step 2. Inspect the Sprockets

If a sprocket has nicks, burrs, gouges, or missing teeth, it should be replaced since sprocket damage can cause the chain to fail. At the same time, the sprockets should be checked for wear. If the sprocket is excessively worn, it should be replaced.

The sprocket should not have any dirt or rust on it, since dirt and rust can cause the chain to wear quickly. A stiff brush can be used to remove any dirt and rust.

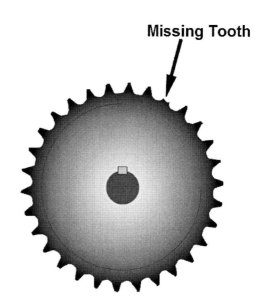

Missing Tooth

Step 3. Mount the Sprockets on the Shafts

The sprockets should be attached to the shafts using either a fixed bore hub or, more commonly, a bushing.

Proper sprocket mounting can be ensured by rotating the shafts and observing the motion of the sprockets, looking for any wobble. If the sprockets wobble, they should be reinstalled or replaced.

Step 4. Mount the Chain

If the chain drive has movable centers, the driver shaft should be adjusted (moved) towards the driven shaft.

This will reduce the center distance between the two sprockets so that the chain can be slipped loosely over the sprockets. Then the chain is placed over the sprockets.

If the drive system does not have movable centers, the chain can be connected and disconnected using a special link called a master link.

Step 5. Align the Sprockets

In order to work most efficiently, the sprockets must be properly aligned. Misaligned sprockets will cause the chain and the bearings to wear quickly.

There are several ways in which sprockets can be misaligned including angular, sprocket, and parallel misalignments. Properly aligned sprockets do not twist or apply excessive forces to the chain.

When aligning sprockets, the shafts must first be leveled using a spirit level. This may have already been performed in step one, when the motor was mounted.

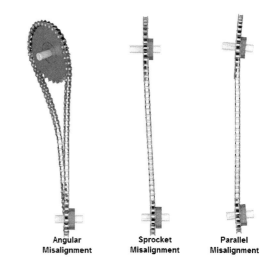

Angular Misalignment   Sprocket Misalignment   Parallel Misalignment

Next, a straight edge is placed against the faces of the sprockets to align the sprocket teeth and check the parallelism of the shafts. If the shafts are parallel and the sprocket teeth are aligned, the faces of the sprockets will be flush against the straight edge.

If a straight edge is not available for this step, a string can be used as well.

Step 6. Apply Tension to the Chain

Proper chain tension is very important to the life of the drive. Some slack is necessary for the chain drive to function properly.

If the tension is too little, the chain will fly off the sprocket. If the tension is too high, the bearings and the chain will wear very quickly.

Tensioning the chain is a 3-step process:

- First, determine the sag needed
- Then, apply tension to the chain
- Finally, measure the sag

Step 7. Apply Lubrication to the Chain

A chain must be lubricated before it can be run. In many cases, new chains will have suitable lubrication for temporary operation.

The easiest way to lubricate a chain is to dip it in an oil bath before installing it. If an oil bath is not available, the chain can be oiled while on the sprockets using an oil can.

Some types of chain drives have a continuous means of lubrication, requiring no operator intervention.

Step 8. Run the Motor Briefly to Test the Drive

Once the chain has been installed, aligned, and lubricated, the motor can be run briefly to ensure that the drive runs smoothly and is fairly quiet.

If so, the drive can continue running. If not, the drive should be stopped and the installation should be checked for problems.

Step 9. Recheck the Chain Sag

After the first 24 hours of operation, the tension in the chain should be rechecked to verify that the chain sag is still adjusted properly.

If the chain tension is still correct, the drive system can be operated full time. If the chain tension is incorrect, it could indicate that something is wrong with the chain drive system.

Chain sag should also be checked at 100 hours of operation and at every 500 hours of operation thereafter.

Step 10. Chain Removal

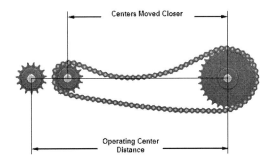

Removing a chain from a drive system with adjustable centers involves simply moving the two shafts closer together. This will create enough slack in the chain so that the chain can easily be lifted off of the sprockets.

If the drive does not have adjustable centers, the master link can be disconnected to allow removal of the chain.

Segment 3   Chain Tensioning

Objective 8   Describe How to Determine Allowable Chain Sag for a Given Application

Chain Slack

In order for a chain to function properly, its tension must be high enough to enable it to stay on the sprockets. However, it must not be so tight as to quickly wear and fail.

For this reason, a chain must have some slack in it, which is called sag. The amount of sag in a chain is an indication of the chain tension.

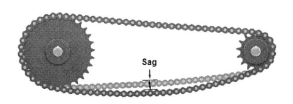

Determining Chain Sag

When a chain is under load, it will have a taut side and a slack side. The taut side is the side of the chain that is being pulled by the driver sprocket.

Chain sag is measured by rotating the sprockets so that there is little or no chain sag in the taut side and then measuring the sag in the slack side.

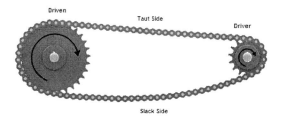

Mid-Span Chain Movement

Chain sag is properly measured at the middle of the span between the two sprockets, which is why it is often called the mid-span sag.

Another term that is often used is the mid-span movement, which is the movement of the sag in both directions. Mid-span movement is always two times the mid-span sag.

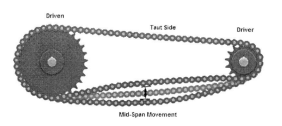

Two Orientations of Chain Drives

The amount of sag a chain drive should have depends on the application of the drive system. The two applications are:

- Vertically Oriented Chain Drives
- Horizontally Oriented Chain Drives

Vertically Oriented Chain Drives

A vertically oriented chain drive is defined as a drive where the angle between the line going through the centers of the two sprockets and a horizontal line is greater than 45°.

The allowable mid-span movement of a vertical chain drive is two to three percent of the distance between sprocket centers.

For example, a vertically oriented chain drive whose distance between centers is 24 inches has an allowable mid-span movement of about 0.6 inch. This corresponds to a mid-span sag of 0.3 inch.

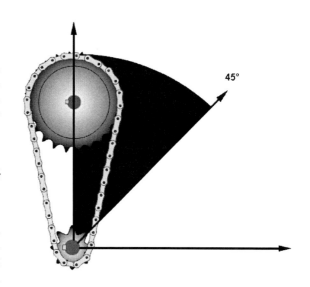

Horizontally Oriented Chain Drives

A horizontally oriented drive is one in which the angle between the line going through the centers of the two sprockets and a horizontal line is less than 45°.

The allowable mid-span movement for a horizontal chain drive is 4 to 6 percent of the distance between sprocket centers.

For example, a horizontal chain drive whose distance between centers is 24 inches has an allowable mid-span movement of about 1.2 inches. This corresponds to a mid-span sag of 0.6 inch.

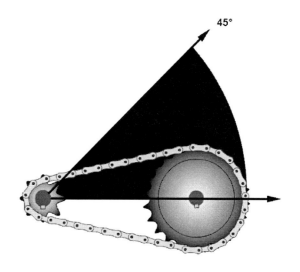

Objective 9   Describe Two Methods Used to Adjust Chain Sag

Two Methods to Adjust Chain Sag

During installation and after the chain has become worn, the chain sag will need to be adjusted. There are two basic methods used to adjust chain sag:

• Adjustable Centers
• Idlers

Adjustable Centers

In a system with adjustable centers, when the sag of a chain needs to be adjusted, the centers of the drive system can be moved either farther apart or closer together.

Idlers

Another method used to adjust chain sag is with a device called a chain idler. A chain idler is a mechanism that has a small sprocket attached to an arm.

Some chain idler arms are spring-loaded, which automatically keeps constant tension in the chain drive via the idler sprocket.

If a spring-loaded arm is not used, the location of the idler sprocket must be manually adjusted to achieve the desired chain tension.

The Wear of a Roller Chain Drive

It is important to understand that adjustment of the chain tension is not due to stretching of the chain. Chains do not stretch. They become longer because they wear.

Specifically, the bushings inside the roller links wear. As these bushings wear, they become smaller, and each link of the chain is pulled farther apart from its neighbors.

This makes it appear as if the chain is stretching, but no individual links are stretching. Only the space between them is increasing.

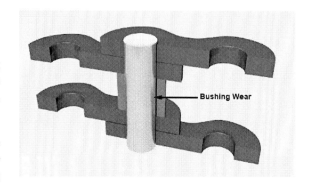

Chain Drive Bearing Wear

The wearing of the bushings is actually a benefit of a chain drive because it allows chains to be used for longer periods of time than other types of drives, and it makes it easy to determine when to replace a chain by measuring its length.

A chain should be replaced when its length becomes 3% longer than its original length.

3% Longer

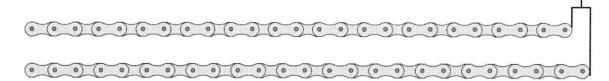

Segment 4   Chain Tension Measurement

Objective 10   Describe How to Measure Chain Sag

Measuring Chain Sag

Before a chain drive can be put into operation, the chain sag must be adjusted. This requires that the actual chain sag be measured using a straight edge and a rule.

To measure chain sag, one sprocket is rotated while the other is held in place. This causes the sag to be on only one side of the drive. A straight edge is then laid across the sprockets on the side with sag.

Midway between the sprockets, the end of a rule is placed on the chain. The sag in the chain is then read off of the rule where it crosses the straight edge.

Segment 5   Fixed Center Chain Installation

Objective 11   Describe the Function and Operation of a Master Link

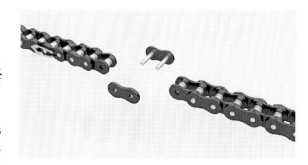

The Purpose of a Master Link

In some mechanical applications, an operator does not have the benefit of adjustable centers.

In other words, the machine's design does not permit the driver shaft or the driven shaft to be moved in order to remove and install chains.

In these cases, a continuous chain loop must be separated so it can be installed and removed.

The Operation of a Master Link

One way to separate and reconnect a chain is to use a special chain link called a master link.

Master links are similar in construction to a standard chain link, but you can remove one side plate.

With the side plate removed, a master link can be inserted into a chain or removed from it.

This allows the chain to be installed onto sprockets. Once the chain is in place, the master link connects the two ends of the chain to form a continuous chain.

A cotter pin or a locking spring clip secures the removable side plate of a master link.

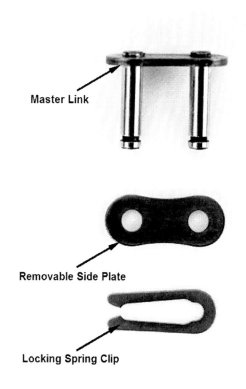

Master Link

Removable Side Plate

Locking Spring Clip

Objective 12 Describe Two Methods of Installing a Lightweight Chain That Uses a Master Link

Two Main Methods

There are two main methods used to install chains that have a master link:

- Using the Sprocket Teeth Mesh
- Using a Chain Puller

Using the Sprocket Teeth Mesh

The simpler of these methods is to use the sprocket teeth mesh. This method involves engaging one end of the chain with one of the sprockets.

The teeth of the sprocket will hold that end in place while the rest of the chain is wrapped around the other sprocket and back to the original end.

When the two ends of the chain are next to each other, the master link can be installed.

Using a Chain Puller

Sometimes, the chain is too heavy or the sprockets have a protective shield over them, preventing the operator from simply using the sprocket teeth mesh to hold one end of the chain in place. In cases like these, a chain puller is used.

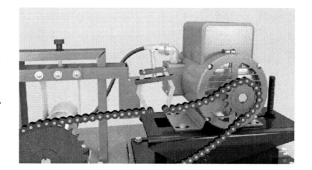

The two ends of a chain are held together using the chain puller while the master link is installed.

Objective 13 Describe the Operation of a Chain Puller

Operation of the Chain Puller

A chain puller operates by pulling the two ends of the chain together with its jaws. The dial on top of the tool opens and closes the jaws. When the jaws are opened far enough, each jaw is inserted into the ends of the chain.

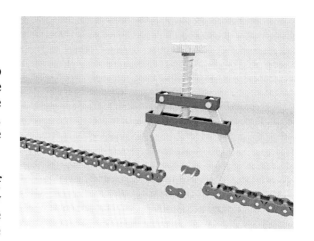

Once the jaws are inserted into the ends of the chain, the chain puller is tightened by turning the dial until the chain ends are close enough to allow the master link to be installed.

Module 6 Spur Gear Drives

Segment 1   Gear Drive Concepts

Objective 1   Describe the Function of the Three Components of a Gear Drive System

Components of a Gear Drive

A gear drive consists of three basic components:

- Driver Gear
- Driven Gear
- Idler Gear

Driver Gear

The driver gear is a disc-shaped component with teeth that is attached to the shaft of the driver.

It is positioned so that its teeth mesh with either the driven gear or the idler gear.

When the drive shaft turns, the driver gear rotates and one or more of its teeth apply a force to the next gear, causing it to rotate.

Driven Gear

The driven gear is a disc-shaped component with teeth that is attached to the driven shaft.

It rotates when the gear next to it rotates and in turn causes the driven shaft to rotate.

Idler Gear

The idler gear is also a disc-shaped component with teeth of the same design as the driver and driven gears.

It is positioned between the driver and driven gears. The idler gear transfers the torque and motion from the driver gear to the driven gear.

Its purpose is to either change the direction of rotation of the driven gear or transfer the power to a location that is farther from the driver shaft. It does not affect either the speed or the torque output of the driven gear.

Delivery of Speed and Torque to the Driven Shaft

The relative diameters of the driver and driven gears determine the speed and torque of the driven shaft.

The ratio of the sizes of the gears is selected to either decrease or increase the speed and torque delivered to the driven shaft.

Types of Gear Drive Designs

A gear drive is designed as either an open or a closed unit.

A closed unit has a housing that contains the gears.

This housing protects the gears and provides a way of containing the oil or grease lubrication.

Open units do not have a housing but still have a guard of some type that is used to contain the lubrication.

Objective 2   Define the Gear Pitch, Pitch Circle, and Pitch Diameter and Explain Their Importance

Definition of Circular Pitch

Like belt drives, the features of pitch circle and pitch diameter are important concepts with gear drives.

Unlike belt drives, however, pitch has a specific meaning in a gear drive.

The pitch of a gear, or circular pitch, is the distance between one point on a tooth and the corresponding point on the next tooth when measured along the pitch circle.

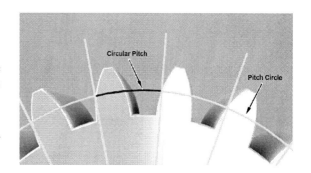

Pitch Circle Description

The pitch circle of a gear is the location on the gear where speed and torque are transmitted.

This occurs at the contact point between the gear teeth along a line that passes through the line of centers of the two gears.

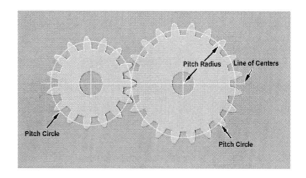

Importance of Pitch Diameter

The pitch diameter is the diameter of the pitch circle and is used to calculate the speed and torque that are transmitted to the driven shaft.

The pitch radius is half of the pitch diameter.

The pitch diameter is important because it can be used to calculate the speed and torque which are transmitted to the driven shaft. The pitch circle is important only because it allows you to determine the pitch diameter.

The term pitch length does not apply to the gear drive, because the gears are in direct contact with each other.

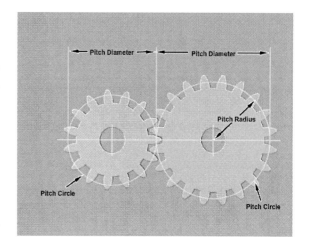

Objective 3   Describe How to Calculate the Gear Ratio of a Gear Drive

Gear Ratio Formulas

The speed and torque that are transmitted to the driven shaft of a gear drive are calculated using the gear ratio, which can be calculated using one of two methods:

- Ratio of Pitch Diameters
- Ratio of Number of Gear Teeth

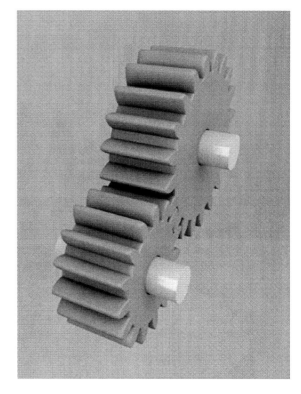

Ratio of Pitch Diameters

The formula shown is used to calculate the gear ratio of a gear drive using the pitch diameters of the gears.

Consider a gear drive system where the pitch diameter of the driver gear is 2 inches and the pitch diameter of the driven gear is 4 inches.

This means that the gear ratio is 2 (GR = 4/2). This gear ratio is also stated as 2:1.

It is important to remember that the gear ratio is determined using the pitch diameter, which is not the same as the outer diameter of a gear. If you use the outer diameter, your answer will have an error.

Gear Ratio Using Pitch Diameters

$$GR = \frac{PD_{DVN}}{PD_{DRV}}$$

Where:

PD_{DRV} = Pitch Diameter of Driver Gear (in)

PD_{DVN} = Pitch Diameter of Driven Gear (in)

GR = Gear Ratio

Insert Known Values:

PD_{DVN} = 4 inches

PD_{DRV} = 2 inches

$$GR = \frac{PD_{DVN}}{PD_{DRV}}$$

Calculate Result:

$$GR = \frac{4}{2}$$

$$GR = 2 = \frac{2}{1} = 2:1$$

Ratio of Number of Gear Teeth

Another method of calculating the gear ratio is to use the number of teeth of each gear, in the formula shown here.

For example, if the driver gear has 11 teeth and the driven gear has 22 teeth, the gear ratio is 2:1.

Ratio of Number of Gear Teeth

$$GR = \frac{N_{DVN}}{N_{DRV}}$$

Where:

GR = Gear Ratio (Teeth)

N_{DVN} = Number of Teeth of Driven Gear

N_{DRV} = Number of Teeth of Driver Gear

Insert Known Values:

$N_{DVN} = 22$

$N_{DVR} = 11$

$$GR = \frac{N_{DVN}}{N_{DVR}}$$

Calculate Result:

$$GR = \frac{22}{11}$$

$$GR = \frac{22}{11} = \frac{2}{1} = 2:1$$

Application of Gear Ratio Formulas

If you are using a manufacturer's catalog data, you can probably use either formula because both the number of teeth and pitch diameter are usually listed.

However, if you are in the plant, you will probably use the ratio of the number of gear teeth because it is easier to count the teeth than measure the pitch diameter.

Description of Gear Ratio

The gear ratio determines how fast the driven gear will turn.

The teeth of the driver gear transfer speed to the teeth of the driven gear such that the points on the teeth of the two gears at their pitch diameters move at the same surface speed.

If the gears are of different sizes, the driven shaft's rotational speed (rpm) will be different from the driver shaft's rotational speed (rpm). The shaft with the larger gear will have a slower rotational speed than the shaft with the small gear.

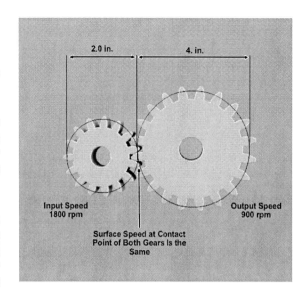

Effect of Gear Ratio

In a similar manner to speed, the gear ratio also affects the torque transmitted to the driven shaft.

Recall that the force applied to the surfaces of the two gears is the same.

Since the torque radius is the pitch radius of the gear, the torque in one gear will be different from another if its radius is different.

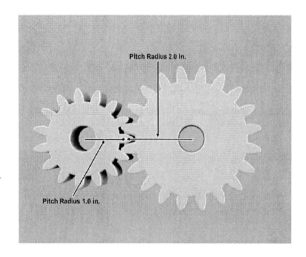

In this example, the effective torque in the driver gear is 10 in.-lbs.

The effective torque in the driven gear, however, is 20 in.-lbs ($T = 10 \times 2 = 20$).

From this discussion, you can say that the larger gear turns slower but has greater torque. This is a common sense concept you can use on the job to determine in general how speed and torque are being changed by the mechanical drive system.

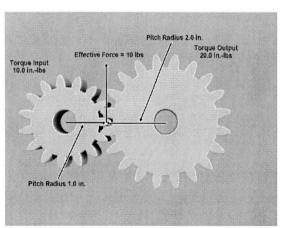

Segment 2 Gear Drive Designs

Objective 4   Describe How to Calculate the Shaft Speed and Torque of a Gear Drive System

Gear Drive Speed Formula

The relationship between gear sizes and shaft speeds of a gear drive can be expressed as shown here.

The shaft speeds are inversely proportional to the pitch diameters and number of teeth.

Therefore, an increase in driven gear size (or teeth) causes its speed to decrease.

Notice that the right-hand side of the formula is actually the gear ratio, so the formula can be restated to include it.

Gear Drive Speed

$$\frac{S_{DRV}}{S_{DVN}} = \frac{PD_{DVN}}{PD_{DRV}}$$

$$\frac{S_{DRV}}{S_{DVN}} = \frac{N_{DVN}}{N_{DRV}}$$

Where:

S_{DVN} = Output Rotational Speed (rpm)

PD_{DVN} = Pitch Diameter of Output Gear (in.)

N_{DRV} = Number of Teeth of Input Gear

N_{DVN} = Number of Teeth of Output Gear

PD_{DRV} = Pitch Diameter of Input Gear (in.)

S_{DRV} = Input Rotational Speed (rpm)

Gear Drive Speed (Using Gear Ratio)

$$\frac{S_{DRV}}{S_{DVN}} = GR$$

Where:

S_{DRV} = Driver Rotational Speed (rpm)

S_{DVN} = Driven Rotational Speed (rpm)

GR = Gear Ratio

Gear Drive Torque Formula

Shaft torque is calculated using a formula that is similar to the shaft speed formula, except the torque is directly, not inversely, proportional to the pitch diameters or the number of teeth.

Gear Drive Torque

$$\frac{T_{DVN}}{T_{DRV}} = \frac{PD_{DVN}}{PD_{DRV}}$$

$$\frac{T_{DVN}}{T_{DRV}} = \frac{N_{DVN}}{N_{DRV}}$$

Where:

T_{DRV} = Input Rotational Torque (in.-lbs)

PD_{DRV} = Pitch Diameter of Input Gear (in.)

N_{DRV} = Number of Teeth of Input Gear

N_{DVN} = Number of Teeth of Output Gear

PD_{DVN} = Pitch Diameter of Output Gear (in.)

T_{DVN} = Output Rotational Torque (in.-lbs)

As with the speed formula, the torque formula can be modified to use the gear ratio.

Gear Drive Torque (Using Gear Ratio)

$$\frac{T_{DVN}}{T_{DRV}} = GR$$

Where:

T_{DVN} = Output Rotational Torque (ft-lb)

T_{DRV} = Input Rotational Torque (ft-lb)

GR = Gear Ratio

Objective 5 — Describe the Functions of Four Types of Gear Drives and Give an Application of Each

Types of Gear Drives

Gear drives come in many designs. One way to group these designs is the direction of orientation of the driven shaft relative to the orientation of the driver shaft. There are four basic categories:

- Parallel Axis
- Intersecting Axis
- Non-Intersecting Axis
- Moving Axis

Parallel Axis

The shafts of a parallel axis gear drive are placed side-by-side or in parallel with each other, as shown here. This is a very common configuration.

A parallel axis gear drive is used in applications where the driven shaft is mounted in the same direction as the driver shaft.

Some machine tools use a parallel axis drive.

Intersecting Axis

The intersecting axis gear drive gets its name because the gears are designed so the axes of the shafts are on the same plane and intersect with each other.

The intersecting axis gear drive is designed to transfer power to a driven shaft that is at a right angle (90°) to the driver shaft.

It is commonly used in applications such as gear reducers.

Non-Intersecting Axis

The non-intersecting gear drive is also designed to transfer power at right angles to the drive shaft, but the axes of the shafts are not on the same plane.

An example of this type of gear is the worm gear or crossed-axis helical gear.

Worm gears are used where there is a need for a low-cost gear reducer with a very high gear ratio.

Moving Axis

The moving axis gear drive is designed to convert rotary motion to linear motion.

One example is the rack and pinion drive.

This is used in fluid power actuators to convert linear motion into rotary motion.

Objective 6 List Four Types of Parallel Shaft Gears and Give an Application of Each

There are four types of gear drives that transfer power between parallel axes:

• Spur
• Helical
• Herringbone
• Internal

Spur

The spur gear drive is the most basic of gear drives. Its teeth are cut into the gear parallel to the axis of rotation.

This type of gear is used mainly in low-to-medium speed applications such as machine tool drives, instrument transducers, and gear reducers because it is low cost and easy to maintain.

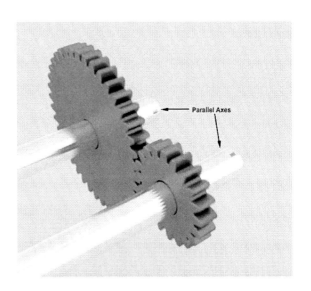

Helical

The helical gear is similar in design to the spur gear except that its teeth are cut into the gear at an angle to the gear's axis of rotation.

This type of gear, while more expensive than the spur gear, is able to operate at higher speeds. It also operates more quietly and smoothly.

One disadvantage to this gear is that it creates a side or thrust load because of its angled gear teeth.

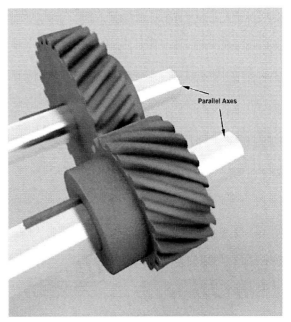

Herringbone

The herringbone gear design is composed of two helical designs. For this reason, it is also called a double helical gear.

This design eliminates the side load caused by the single helical design, because the side loads of the two helical gears cancel each other out.

Herringbone gears are used for applications that require quiet, high-speed, heavy-load operation.

An example is the power take-off of a gas turbine.

The name herringbone comes from the gear's resemblance to the spine of a fish.

Internal

Gears can be classified as either internal or external. This describes how the teeth are oriented on the gear.

The internal gear drive uses one or more external gears to drive a larger internal gear. This type of gear drive is used when a very large gear ratio is needed but the axes must be parallel and the gear drive must be compact.

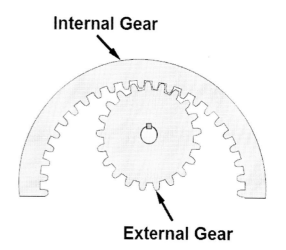

Internal Gear

External Gear

One example of an internal gear drive is a planetary gear drive. This type uses small gears called planets, which revolve around a central gear called a sun gear.

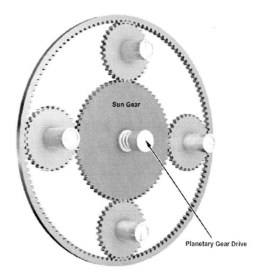

Planetary Gear Drive

Another type of internal gear drive is a harmonic gear drive. This type of drive consists of a flexible external gear ring which is forced out against an internal ring gear by an elliptical-shaped wave generator. As the wave generator rotates, the flexible gear drives the internal ring gear.

It is commonly used in precision applications such as robot axes because it has no backlash or play in the gears.

Harmonic Gear Drive

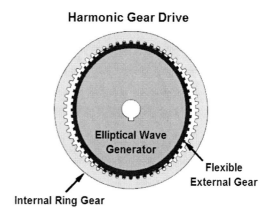

Internal Ring Gear

Segment 3   Spur Gear Operation

Objective 7   Describe Eleven Features of a Gear

Description of Gear Features

Because gears mesh directly with each other, the shape and dimensions of gear teeth are very important.

In order to understand the operation of meshing gear teeth, you must first learn the features of a gear.

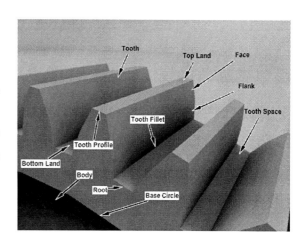

- Tooth
- Tooth Space
- Body
- Face
- Flank
- Tooth Profile
- Root
- Tooth Fillet
- Top Land
- Bottom Land
- Base Circle

Tooth

The tooth is the part of the gear that makes contact with the other gear to transmit torque and speed.

Tooth Space

The tooth space is the volume of space between two teeth of the gear.

Body

The body is the part of the gear that does not have teeth.

Face

The face is the surface area of the tooth that is above the pitch circle.

Flank

The flank is the surface area of the tooth that is below the pitch circle.

Tooth Profile

The tooth profile is the shape made by the edge of the tooth.

Root

The root is the point on the profile of the tooth where the profile starts.

Tooth Fillet

The tooth fillet is the line on the tooth edge that blends with the root.

Top Land

The top land is the surface area that is on top of the tooth.

Bottom Land

The bottom land is the surface area that is on the bottom of the tooth.

Base Circle

The base circle is a circle from which the profile of the teeth is created.

Objective 8   Identify the Twelve Dimensions of a Gear and Explain the Importance of Each

Dimensions of a Gear

You have already learned the meanings of three important gear dimensions: pitch, pitch circle, and pitch diameter.

These are some other important dimensions of a gear:

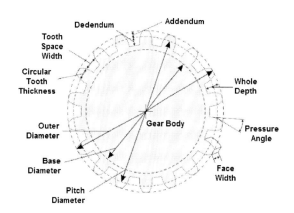

- Face Width
- Circular Tooth Thickness
- Tooth Space Width
- Pressure Angle
- Outer Diameter
- Base Circle Diameter
- Addendum
- Dedendum
- Whole Depth
- Number of Teeth
- Pitch Diameter
- Diametral Pitch

Face Width

The face width is the width as measured across the face of the gear.

This is an important dimension because it specifies gear size.

A thicker gear is needed for higher loads.

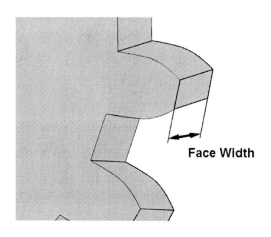

Face Width

Circular Tooth Thickness

The circular tooth thickness is measured along the pitch circle from one side of a tooth to the other.

It can also be measured in a straight line between the two points on the pitch circle, in which case it is called the chordal thickness.

The tooth thickness is important for inspection of gear wear. As gears wear, the thickness becomes smaller.

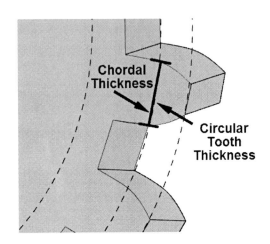

Tooth Space Width

The width of a tooth space is the length between two adjacent teeth as measured along the pitch circle.

It is important because it must be larger than the tooth thickness in order to allow the gears to mesh smoothly.

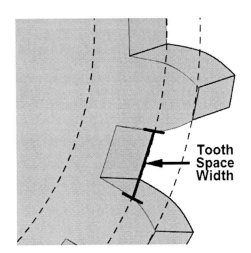

Pressure Angle

The pressure angle can be described as the angle between a line that is tangent to the tooth profile at the pitch circle and a radial line extending from the center of the gear.

The pressure angle affects how the gears transmit power between each other.

In general, a higher pressure angle gives better operation because it does not wear as quickly, it can carry higher loads, and it allows higher speeds.

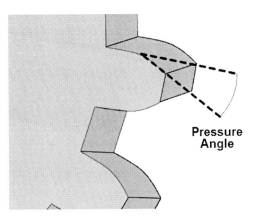

Two common pressure angles are in use today: 14.5° and 20°. The 20° angle is most often found on new machinery, while the 14.5° is very common on older machinery.

It is important to note that two gears must have the same pressure angle in order to be used with each other.

You cannot mesh gears of different pressure angles together.

Outer Diameter

The outer diameter is the diameter of the circle that is drawn through the top lands of the teeth.

The outer diameter is not used for calculations but it is important for two reasons.

First, it is necessary for design of clearance for other machine elements, such as covers.

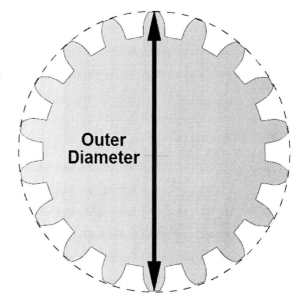

Additionally, it is easily measured and can be used to determine a dimension called the diametral pitch.

The diametral pitch is used to size the gear.

This is very helpful when you need to replace a gear on a machine.

Base Circle Diameter

The base circle diameter, or simply base diameter, is important because it is the basis for many other gear dimensions.

However, you will not use this dimension unless you are designing gears.

The base radius is equal to half of the base diameter.

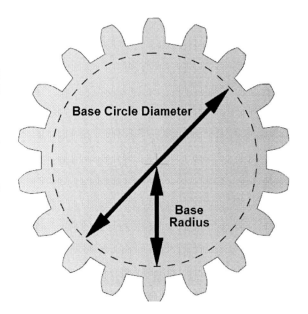

Addendum

The addendum is the distance from the pitch circle to the top land. It coincides with the tooth face.

Some spur gears are made with addendums that are shorter than normal. These are called stub tooth gears.

The addendum is important only if you are designing or making gears.

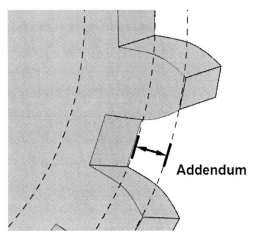

Dedendum

The dedendum is the distance from the pitch circle to the bottom land.

It is the length of the tooth flank.

The dedendum is important only if you are designing or making gears.

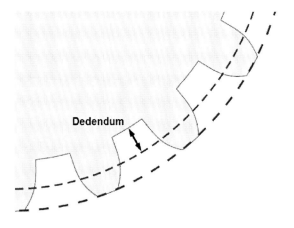

Whole Depth

The whole depth is the sum of the dedendum and the addendum.

The whole depth is important only if you are designing or making gears.

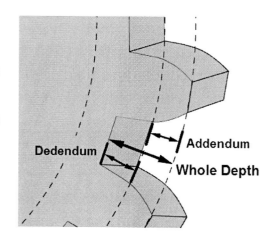

Number of Teeth

The number of teeth on the gear is used to calculate the gear ratio of the two gears so that the speed and torque output of the drive can be determined.

It is also used on the shop floor to calculate the diametral pitch which is used to specify replacement gears.

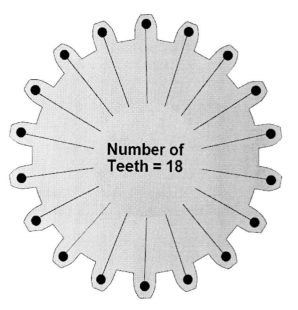

Pitch Diameter

The pitch diameter is the diameter of the pitch circle.

It is important because it defines the size of the gear and is used to calculate the speed and torque that is transmitted from one gear to another.

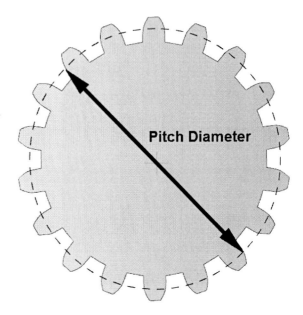

Diametral Pitch

The diametral pitch is the ratio of the number of teeth on the gear to the pitch diameter.

It indicates the relative size of the teeth on the gear.

Two gears must have the same diametral pitch in order to mesh.

Diametral Pitch

$$P = \frac{N}{PD}$$

Where:

PD = Pitch Diameter (inches)

N = Number of Teeth

P = Diametral Pitch

The diametral pitch allows you to determine if gears of different diameters or different numbers of teeth have the same size teeth and therefore can mesh properly.

Later you will learn a simple method to determine the diametral pitch of a gear by measuring the outer diameter.

This is very helpful when you need to replace a gear on the shop floor.

Objective 9   Identify the Ten Dimensions and Features of a Gear Drive and Explain the Importance of Each

Dimensions and Features of a Gear Drive System

Now that you know the features and dimensions of a single gear, the next step is to learn about the key dimensions and features of two gears that mesh with each other.

- Pinion
- Bull Gear
- Line of Centers
- Center Distance
- Line of Action
- Pressure Angle
- Pitch Point
- Clearance
- Working Depth
- Backlash

Pinion

When the gears are of different sizes, the smaller gear is called the pinion.

The pinion can be attached to either the driver or the driven shafts, depending on the change in output torque and speed desired.

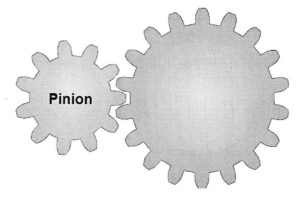

Bull Gear

When the gears are of different sizes, the larger gear is called the bull gear or simply the gear.

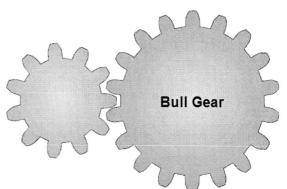

Line of Centers

The line of centers is the line that passes through the centers of the two gears.

It is used as a reference for a number of dimensions such as center distance and pressure angle.

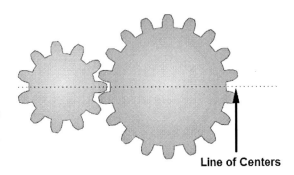

Line of Centers

Center Distance

The center distance is the distance between the centers of the gears.

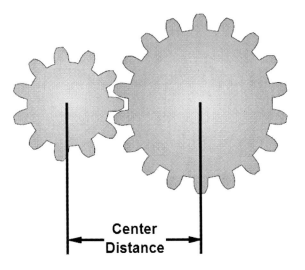

Center Distance

Line of Action

The line of action is the path made by the point where the two gears make contact.

For an involute profile, this path follows a line that is tangent to the two base circles.

It helps to determine the pressure angle.

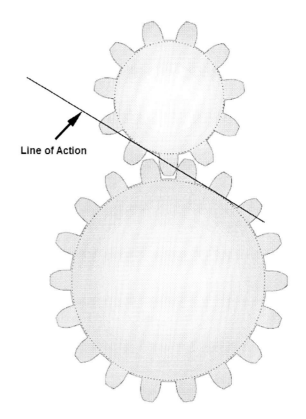

Line of Action

Pressure Angle

The pressure angle is the angle between the line of action and a line that is perpendicular to the line of centers.

It is a feature of the gear tooth profile.

The pressure angle of the gear tooth profile is generated based on this pressure angle.

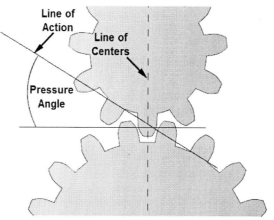

The pressure angle made by the line of action depends on the distance between the gears.

The actual angle is called the operating pressure angle. The angle to which the gear profile is cut is called the generating pressure angle.

If the gear positions are adjusted correctly, the operating pressure angle should be the same as the generating pressure angle.

Pitch Point

The pitch point is the point where the line of centers and the line of action cross.

The pitch point determines the diameter of the pitch circle for each of the two gears.

Since the pressure angle determines where the line of action crosses the line of centers, the pitch diameter of a gear is determined by the pressure angle and the base circle.

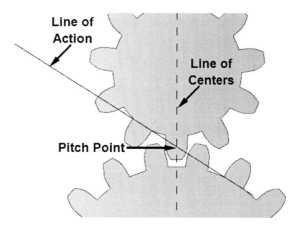

The pitch point, where the line of action crosses the line of centers, is affected by the distance between centers because this causes the pressure angle to change.

Therefore, the actual pitch circles of the gears depend in part on the center distance of the gears.

As with the pressure angle, the actual pitch circle determined by both the base circles and the center distance is called the operating pitch circle. The pitch circle determined by the base circle and the generating pressure angle is called the generating pitch circle.

Clearance

The clearance is the space between the top land of a tooth and the bottom land of the space between the teeth with which the tooth meshes.

It is important to have some clearance in order to keep the tooth of each gear from jamming into bottom lands of each other.

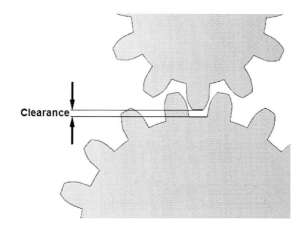

Working Depth

The working depth is the amount by which the meshing teeth engage each other.

It is the distance between the top land of one tooth and the top land of the tooth with which it meshes. This is equal to the whole depth minus the clearance.

The working depth must be less than the whole depth or the gears will interfere with each other.

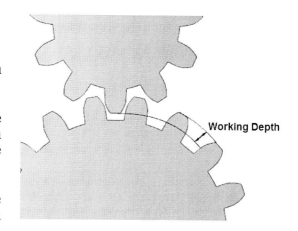

Backlash

Backlash is the difference between the thickness of a tooth and the width of the tooth space.

Most gears have some backlash built into them to allow the gears to mesh smoothly.

This backlash is made by making the tooth thickness slightly smaller than the tooth width.

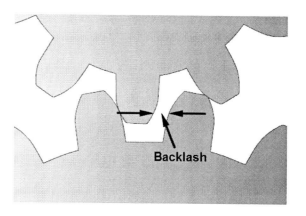

Objective 10 Describe the Operation of a Spur Gear Drive

Spur Gear Drive Description

A spur gear drive transfers the power between two parallel shafts by placing the centers of the two gears close enough together to cause the teeth to mesh.

As the driver gear rotates, its teeth will contact the teeth of the driven gear.

The interaction between these teeth is a combination of rolling and sliding, causing the driven gear to rotate.

The Law of Gearing

The gear teeth of a spur gear are cut parallel to the axis of rotation so that each tooth of the driver gear contacts the tooth of the driven gear across its entire face width.

For basic transmission of force and motion, the gear teeth do not need to have any particular shape.

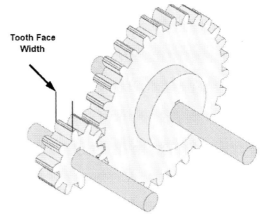

Tooth Face Width

However, for quiet and vibrationless motion, the rotational speeds of the two gears must remain constant as the gears turn.

This will occur if a line, which is perpendicular to both of the tooth profiles at the point of contact, passes through a constant point on the line of centers while the two teeth remain in contact.

This is called the Fundamental Law of Gearing and the point through which the normal line passes is called the pitch point.

Any two gears that have teeth that satisfy the Law of Gearing will have constant pitch diameters and therefore a constant ratio of speed and torque. This type of motion is referred to as conjugate action.

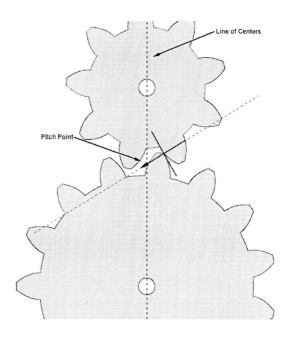

Involute Tooth Profile Advantages

There are actually many types of tooth profiles that satisfy the Law of Gearing. Two of these are involute and cycloidal.

Most spur gears use the involute tooth design.

This profile not only satisfies the Law of Gearing but also provides other advantages:

- Conjugate Action Is Independent of Center Distance
- Straight Tooth Rack
- One Cutter

Involute Tooth Profile

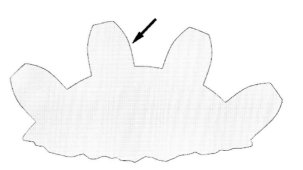

Conjugate Action Is Independent of Center Distance

Conjugate action is independent of center distance means that the gears do not have to be perfectly positioned with their pitch circles tangent to each other in order to maintain a constant speed ratio.

In other words, the amount of backlash does not affect the speed ratio.

Straight Tooth Rack

The involute tooth profile becomes straight when it is laid out on a linear rack.

This makes involute tooth design easy to manufacture.

One Cutter

One cutter can generate all gear tooth numbers of the same diametral pitch.

Effects of an Involute Profile

Another benefit of the involute tooth shape, which is also shared by some of the other tooth shapes, is that the teeth tend to roll more than they slip. This reduces friction and helps the gears to operate smoothly.

Notice that the gear teeth have an involute design on both sides so that the gears can drive in either direction.

Backlash Description

Spur gears are designed with a small amount of clearance between the backside of the driver gear tooth and front of the driven tooth. This clearance is called backlash. It is created by making the teeth slightly smaller than the tooth spaces.

Backlash is needed in order to allow lubricant to get to each gear tooth and to allow the teeth to mesh properly. It is important that the backlash is neither too much nor too little.

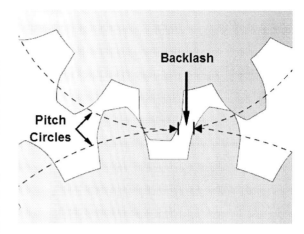

Spur Gear Construction

Spur gears are made of many different materials including cast iron, forged steel, machined steel, brass, bronze, and even plastic. Cast iron has good resistance to wear but is brittle.

Unhardened low-carbon steel is sometimes used on low power applications, but it must be hardened for higher power applications like those commonly seen in industry.

Spur gears are designed to be mounted with either fixed bores with keyways or with bushings.

Segment 4 Spur Gear Installation

Objective 11 Describe How to Install and Align a Spur Gear Drive System

Spur Gear Installation and Alignment

In many cases, installation of a spur gear drive is very easy because the gear drive design uses shaft bearings that have a fixed mounting.

This fixes the locations of the gears, and therefore no alignment is necessary.

However, some gear drives are designed for backlash adjustment. These types of drives must be aligned.

The general procedure for installing a gear drive is an 8-step process.

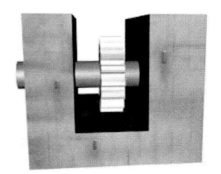

- Step 1. Mount and Level the Motor and the Driven Component
- Step 2. Inspect the Gears for Cleanliness and Wear
- Step 3. Mount the Gears onto the Shafts
- Step 4. Mesh the Gears
- Step 5. Align the Gears
- Step 6. Adjust the Backlash
- Step 7. Readjust Alignment and Tighten Bolts
- Step 8. Apply Lubrication

Step 1. Mount and Level the Motor and the Driven Component

The shafts must be level so that the gear teeth contact each other across their entire width.

The shafts should also be checked for run-out and a soft foot.

Run-out will cause the shaft to wobble making the gear teeth mesh improperly.

This causes the gears to wear quickly.

Ideally, the shaft run-out should be no more than 0.002 inch.

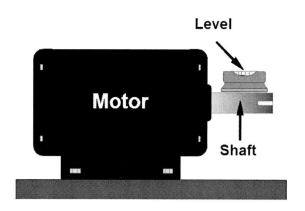

Step 2. Inspect the Gears for Cleanliness and Wear

If a gear has nicks, burrs, gouges, or is excessively worn, replace the gear.

Make sure that the gear is free from dirt.

Dirt can be mixed with the oil lubricating the gears and become deposited on the teeth.

Use a stiff brush to remove dirt from the gear and then wipe it clean.

Step 3. Mount the Gears onto the Shafts

The gears are attached to the shafts using a bushing or a finished bore hub and a key fastener.

Step 4. Mesh the Gears

Move the shafts together so that the gears mesh.

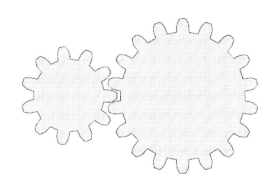

Adjust the position of the gear's shaft so there is a little backlash in the gears.

In step 6, you will adjust their position precisely.

If the shaft centers are fixed, this step is not necessary.

Step 5. Align the Gears

Just as with V-belts and chain drives, it is important to align gears.

Misalignment will cause the gears to either wear or fail.

The gears can be aligned by first leveling the two shafts using a spirit level.

The next step is to place a straight edge against the faces of the gears and check the parallelism of the shafts.

The faces of the gears should be made so that they are flush against the straight edge.

This means the shafts are parallel and the gears are aligned.

Types of Misalignment

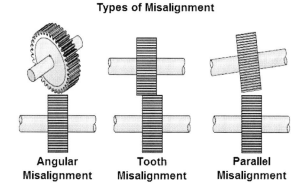

Angular Misalignment   Tooth Misalignment   Parallel Misalignment

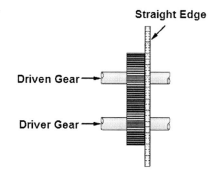

Straight Edge

Driven Gear →

Driver Gear →

Step 6. Adjust the Backlash

It is important that the backlash is set to the proper amount. It should be neither too much nor too little.

The amount of backlash is determined using either a table or a formula.

It can be measured using a dial indicator and is adjusted by moving the centers of the shafts either closer or farther apart.

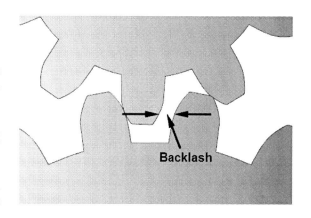

Step 7. Readjust Alignment and Tighten Bolts

After the positions of the shafts have been set, the mounting bolts can be tightened.

As you do this, use a straight edge to keep the alignment of the gears.

After you have tightened the bolts, check the alignment one more time to ensure the gears are still aligned.

Tightening the mounting hardware can often shift the alignment of the shafts.

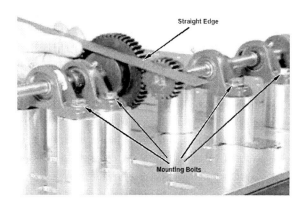

Step 8. Apply Lubrication

Metal gears must be lubricated. In most cases, you will use a type of oil called gear oil, which is made for gear lubrication.

This oil can be applied by hand or with some type of automatic system.

Objective 12   Describe the Function of Backlash

Backlash Description

Backlash is defined as the clearance between the back of the engaged tooth of the driver gear and the front of the tooth of the driven gear immediately behind it as measured along the pitch circle.

A certain amount of backlash is needed in a gear drive to enable the gears to mesh smoothly and to allow lubrication to get to each tooth.

If the backlash is too small, there will be more friction between the gears, which will cause the gears to run roughly, have added load due to friction, wear out quickly, and even lock up.

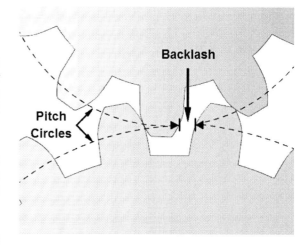

Excessive Backlash

It is also important to not have too much backlash.

This causes the gears to make more noise and vibration, create excessive wear on the faces of the teeth, and even cause the teeth to break.

Some backlash is built into gears by making the teeth slightly narrower than the spaces between the teeth.

Adjusting Backlash

If new gears are adjusted so that their pitch circles are tangent with each other, the gears will have the correct amount of backlash.

Backlash can be changed by adjusting positions of the gears' shaft centers.

As the center distance is increased, the backlash becomes greater.

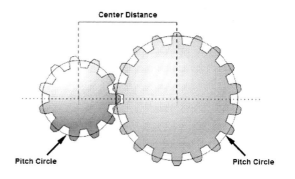

Objective 13 Describe How to Determine the Allowable Backlash in a Gear Drive

Allowable Backlash Range

Whether gears are new or used, the backlash should remain within a certain range in order to operate smoothly with minimum wear on the teeth.

This allowable range of backlash for any two gears can be determined using a table if you know the diametral pitch and the center distance.

This table was developed by the American Gear Manufacturers' Association (AGMA) and is published in the Machinery's Handbook, as well as in other sources.

Center Distance (inches)	Coarse - Pitch Gears				
	Normal Diametral Pitches				
	0.5-1.99	2-3.49	3.5-5.99	6-9.99	10-19.99
Up to 5					0.005-0.015
Over 5 to 10				0.010-0.020	0.010-0.020
Over 10 to 20			0.020-0.030	0.015-0.025	0.010-0.020
Over 20 to 30		0.030-0.040	0.025-0.030	0.025-0.030	
Over 30 to 40	0.040-0.060	0.035-0.045	0.030-0.040	0.025-0.040	
Over 40 to 50	0.050-0.070	0.040-0.055	0.035-0.050	0.030-0.040	
Over 50 to 80	0.060-0.080	0.045-0.085	0.040-0.060		
Over 80 to 100	0.070-0.095	0.050-0.080			
Over 100 to 120	0.080-0.10				

Calculating Diametral Pitch and Center Distance

The diametral pitch can be determined using either a table or by calculating it if you have the number of teeth and the pitch diameter.

The center distance is the average of the sum of the two pitch diameters.

Diametral Pitch

$$P = \frac{N}{PD}$$

Where:

PD = Pitch Diameter (inches)

N = Number of Teeth

P = Diametral Pitch

Center Distance

$$C = \frac{PD_{G1} + PD_{G2}}{2}$$

Where:

PD_{G2} = Pitch Diameter of Gear 2 (inches)

PD_{G1} = Pitch Diameter of Gear 1 (inches)

C = Center Distance (inches)

Positioning New Gears

For new gears, they can be positioned correctly by measuring the backlash.

If it is within the allowable range, the gears are positioned with the pitch circles very close to being tangent to one another.

This method is often easier than measuring the center distance.

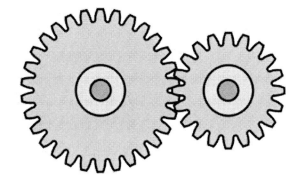

Segment 5   Spur Gear Analysis

Objective 14   Describe Two Methods of Measuring Spur Gear Backlash

Backlash Measurement Methods

The actual backlash between two spur gears can be measured using one of these two methods:

• Direct Dial Indicator Measurement
• Indirect Dial Indicator Measurement

With both of these methods, the basic concept used to perform the measurement is to hold one gear fixed and rotate the other gear back and forth.

The amount of movement of the teeth at or near the pitch circle is the backlash.

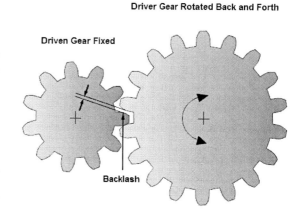

Driver Gear Rotated Back and Forth

Driven Gear Fixed

Backlash

Direct Dial Indicator Measurement

With the direct method, the probe of a dial indicator is placed directly on a tooth and oriented perpendicular to the face of the tooth.

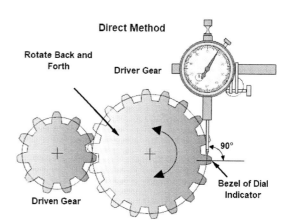

Direct Method

Rotate Back and Forth

Driver Gear

90°

Bezel of Dial Indicator

Driven Gear

Indirect Dial Indicator Measurement

With the indirect method, a bar of some type is attached to the shaft and the indicator measures its movement.

To determine the backlash, you must divide the measured value by the ratio of the distance along the bar from the shaft center to the indicator point to the pitch radius.

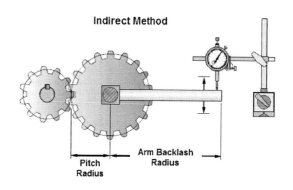

Indirect Method

Pitch Radius

Arm Backlash Radius

Method Application

The direct method is most often used for larger gears where the teeth are large enough to allow the indicator probe to contact a tooth.

The indirect method is used where either the gears are not easy to access or the gear teeth are very small.

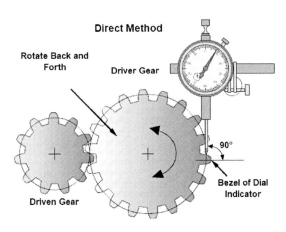

Direct Method

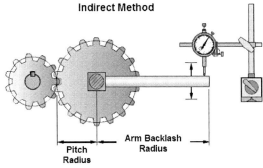

Indirect Method

Module 7 Multiple Shaft Drives

Segment 1   Multiple Shaft Gear Analysis

Objective 1   Describe How to Calculate the Speed and Torque Output in a Multiple Shaft Gear Drive

Multiple Shaft Gear Drives

Gear drives can have more than two gears in the gear train. These additional gears either act as idlers or drive an additional output shaft.

Idler gears are used mainly to change the direction of rotation or to transfer the power to a shaft that is located farther away from the driver shaft.

An example of a multiple output shaft gear drive is the lathe. For each shaft driven, a separate gear is needed.

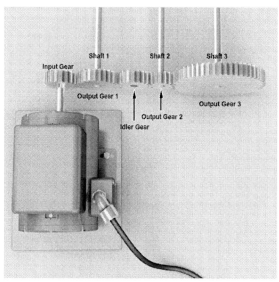

Canceling Effect of Idler Gears

It is first important to note that idler gears do not affect the torque or the speed of the driven shaft.

If you were to calculate the gear ratio by multiplying the ratios of each pair of neighboring gears together, the effect of the idler gears is canceled out.

Notice that the number of teeth of both idler gears is used twice in the formula. They cancel each other out as shown.

You would get the same gear ratio if you calculated the gear ratio without accounting for the idler gears.

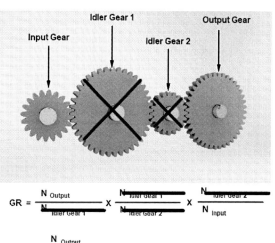

$$GR = \frac{N_{Output}}{N_{\text{Idler Gear 1}}} \times \frac{N_{\text{Idler Gear 1}}}{N_{\text{Idler Gear 2}}} \times \frac{N_{\text{Idler Gear 2}}}{N_{Input}}$$

$$GR = \frac{N_{Output}}{N_{Input}}$$

Speed and Torque in Multiple Shaft Gear Drive

Whether an extra gear in a gear train is an idler or drives an extra shaft, the method used to determine the speed and torque output of a gear drive with more than two gears is the same.

Since the idler gears do not affect the gear ratio, they do not affect the speed or torque.

The same formulas used to calculate the speed and torque of two gears can therefore be used to calculate the output of a gear drive with multiple gears.

Gear Ratio and Speed

$$GR = \frac{S_i}{S_o}$$

Where:

GR = Gear Ratio

S_i = Speed of Input Gear (rpm)

S_o = Speed of Output Gear (rpm)

Gear Drive Torque (Using Gear Ratio)

$$\frac{T_{DVN}}{T_{DRV}} = GR$$

Where:

T_{DVN} = Output Rotational Torque (ft-lb)

T_{DRV} = Input Rotational Torque (ft-lb)

GR = Gear Ratio

Multiple Shaft Example: Gear Ratio Formula

The speed of any driven gear is therefore determined by calculating the gear ratio using the driven gear as the output gear along with the input gear and ignoring all other gears in between.

For example, the gear drive shown has three output gears, each of which drives a separate shaft with a separate load. It also has one true idler gear.

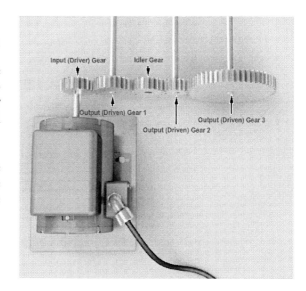

Output Gear 1 (30 Teeth)

Gear Ratio for Gear 1

$$GR_{OG1} = \frac{N_{OG1}}{N_{IG}}$$

$$GR_{OG1} = \frac{30}{20}$$

$$\boxed{GR_{OG1} = 1.5}$$

Output Gear 2 (10 Teeth)

Gear Ratio for Gear 2

$$GR_{OG2} = \frac{N_{OG2}}{N_{IG}}$$

$$GR_{OG2} = \frac{10}{20}$$

$$\boxed{GR_{OG2} = 0.5}$$

Output Gear 3 (60 Teeth)

Gear Ratio for Gear 3

$$GR_{OG3} = \frac{N_{OG3}}{N_{IG}}$$

$$GR_{OG3} = \frac{60}{20}$$

$$\boxed{GR_{OG3} = 3}$$

Multiple Shaft Example: Speed Calculation

The speed of each output shaft can now be calculated separately using its own gear ratio.

The idler gear has no effect on the speed of any output shaft.

In addition, the speed of one output shaft has no effect on the speed of the other output shafts because they act like idlers with respect to the other shafts.

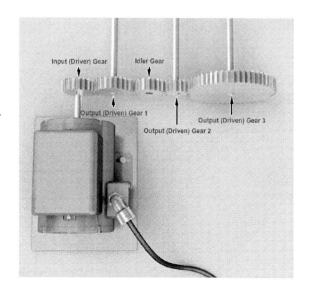

Output Gear 1

Output Speed for Gear 1

$$S_{OG1} = \frac{S_{IG}}{GR_{OG1}}$$

$$S_{OG1} = \frac{60}{1.5}$$

$$\boxed{S_{OG1} = 40 \text{ rpm}}$$

Output Gear 2

Output Speed for Gear 2

$$S_{OG2} = \frac{S_{IG}}{GR_{OG2}}$$

$$S_{OG2} = \frac{60}{0.5}$$

$$\boxed{S_{OG2} = 120 \text{ rpm}}$$

Output Gear 3

Output Speed for Gear 3

$$S_{OG3} = \frac{S_{IG}}{GR_{OG3}}$$

$$S_{OG3} = \frac{60}{3}$$

$$\boxed{S_{OG3} = 20 \text{ rpm}}$$

Multiple Shaft Example: Torque Calculation

The total torque required from the input shaft is calculated by summing the torques that would be required to drive each output shaft by itself.

The torque created at the driver shaft by each output shaft is found by dividing the output torque by the gear ratio.

For example, the torque created at the driver shaft by gear 3 is found by dividing shaft 3's output torque by its gear ratio.

The same goes for the torque created by shaft 2 and shaft 1.

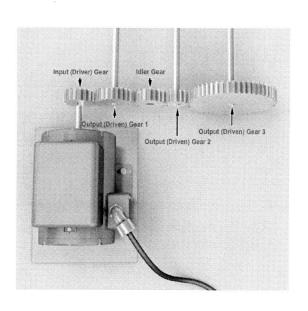

Output Gear 1 (30 in.-lb)

Required Torque for Gear 1

$$T1_{IG} = \frac{T_{OG1}}{GR_{OG1}}$$

$$T1_{IG} = \frac{30}{1.5}$$

$$\boxed{T1_{IG} = 20 \text{ in.-lb}}$$

Output Gear 2 (15 in.-lb)

Required Torque for Gear 2

$$T2_{IG} = \frac{T_{OG2}}{GR_{OG2}}$$

$$T2_{IG} = \frac{15}{0.5}$$

$$\boxed{T2_{IG} = 30 \text{ in.-lb}}$$

Output Gear 3 (20 in.-lb)

Required Torque for Gear 3

$$T3_{IG} = \frac{T_{OG3}}{GR_{OG3}}$$

$$T3_{IG} = \frac{20}{3}$$

$$\boxed{T3_{IG} = 6.7 \text{ in.-lb}}$$

Multiple Shaft Example: Total Torque Calculation

The total torque created on the driver shaft is then calculated by summing the individual torques.

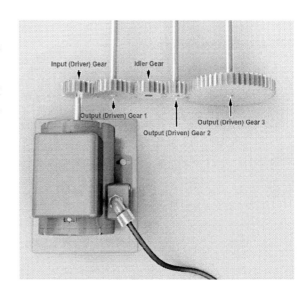

Input Gear

Total Required Torque

$$T_{IG} = T1_{IG} + T2_{IG} + T3_{IG}$$

$$T_{IG} = 20 + 30 + 6.7$$

$$T_{IG} = 20 + 36.7$$

$$\boxed{T_{IG} = 56.7 \text{ in.-lb}}$$

Objective 2 Describe the Function of a Compound Gear Drive System and Give an Application

Compound Gear Drive Description

A compound gear drive is a type of gear train that has two or more gears mounted on one shaft.

These gears can be mounted anywhere on the shaft, either next to each other or on opposite ends of the shaft.

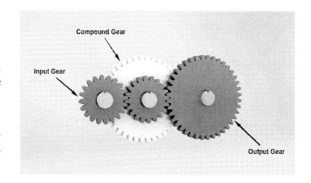

Compound Gear Drive Application

Compound gear drives are used in several types of applications.

Two such applications are driving two output shafts at different speeds and driving an output shaft that is offset from the driver shaft.

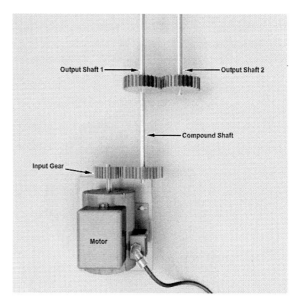

Description of a Reverted Gear Drive

A third type of application for the compound gear drive is to create a gear reduction between two shafts, which are located on the same axis.

This is called a reverted gear drive.

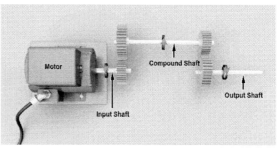

Objective 3   Describe How to Calculate the Torque and Speed Output of a Compound Gear Drive System

Include Compound Gear Ratios to Calculate Speed

The concepts that were used to calculate speed and torque of simple multiple-gear gear drives can also be applied to compound gear drives with one minor change.

The gear ratio of any gears that are mounted on the same shaft must be included in the calculation.

In effect, these gear ratios must be combined as shown.

Compound Gear Drive Speed and Pitch Circle Diameter

$$\frac{S_{DVR}}{S_{DVN}} = \frac{PCD_{DVN}}{PCD_{DVR}} \times \frac{PCD_{ci}}{PCD_{co}}$$

Where:

S_{DVR} = Speed of Driver Gear

S_{DVN} = Speed of Driven Gear

PCD_{DVN} = Pitch Circle Diameter of Driven Gear

PCD_{DVR} = Pitch Circle Diameter of Driver Gear

PCD_{ci} = Pitch Circle Diameter of Compound Input Gear

PCD_{co} = Pitch Circle Diameter of Compound Output Gear

Calculate Speed Using Number of Teeth

The formulas for speed are the same as the simple gear drive except that they are multiplied by the gear ratio of the compound gears.

This ratio can also be calculated using the number of teeth.

Like a simple gear drive, idler gears have no effect on the output speed.

Compound Gear Drive Speed Using Number of Teeth

$$\frac{S_{DVR}}{S_{DVN}} = \frac{N_{DVN}}{N_{DVR}} \times \frac{N_{ci}}{N_{co}}$$

Where:

S_{DVR} = Speed of Driver Gear

S_{DVN} = Speed of Driven Gear

N_{DVN} = Number of Teeth on Driven Gear

N_{DVR} = Number of Teeth on Driver Gear

N_{ci} = Number of Teeth on Compound Input Gear

N_{co} = Number of Teeth on Compound Output Gear

Example of Speed Calculation

To give an example of how these formulas work, look at the compound gear drive shown.

In this case, the gear ratio of the driven gears to the driver gears is 3:1 and the gear ratio of the compound gears is 1:2.

This means the combined or compound gear ratio is 3:2.

The speed of the output gear is therefore 1200 rpm given an input speed of 1800 rpm.

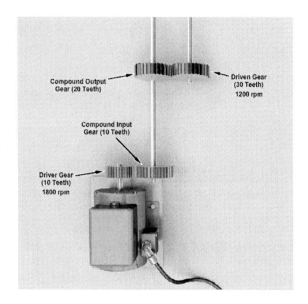

Driven-to-Driver Gear Ratio

$$\frac{N_{DVN}}{N_{DVR}}$$

Where:

N_{DVN} = Number of Teeth on Driven Gear

N_{DVR} = Number of Teeth on Driver Gear

$$\frac{30}{10} = \frac{3}{1} = 3{:}1$$

Ratio of Compound Gears

$$\frac{N_{ci}}{N_{co}}$$

Where:

N_{ci} = Number of Teeth on Compound Input Gear

N_{co} = Number of Teeth on Compound Output Gear

$$\frac{10}{20} = \frac{1}{2} = 1{:}2$$

Combined Gear Ratio

$$\frac{N_{DVN}}{N_{DVR}} \times \frac{N_{ci}}{N_{co}}$$

Where:

N_{DVN} = Number of Teeth on Driven Gear

N_{DVR} = Number of Teeth on Driver Gear

N_{ci} = Number of Teeth on Compound Input Gear

N_{co} = Number of Teeth on Compound Output Gear

$$\frac{30}{10} \times \frac{10}{20} = \frac{30}{20} = 3:2$$

Output Speed

$$\frac{S_{DVR}}{S_{DVN}} = \frac{N_{DVN}}{N_{DVR}} \times \frac{N_{ci}}{N_{co}}$$

$$\frac{1,800}{S_{DVN}} = \frac{30}{10} \times \frac{10}{20}$$

$$\frac{1,800}{S_{DVN}} = \frac{3}{2}$$

$$S_{DVN} = \frac{2}{3} \times 1,800$$

$$\boxed{S_{DVN} = 1,200 \text{ rpm}}$$

Double Reduction Gear Drive Description

The drive shown here is called a double reduction gear drive because it reduces the speed using the combination of two gear ratios.

A triple reduction would use three gear ratios and have two compound gear sets.

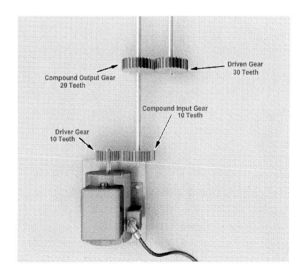

Driven Gear 30 Teeth

Compound Output Gear 20 Teeth

Compound Input Gear 10 Teeth

Driver Gear 10 Teeth

Combine Gear Ratios to Calculate Torque

In a similar way, the torque output is also determined by combining the two gear ratios.

Compound Gear Drive Torque and Pitch Circle Diameter

$$\frac{T_{DVN}}{T_{DVR}} = \frac{PCD_{DVN}}{PCD_{DVR}} \times \frac{PCD_{ci}}{PCD_{co}}$$

Where:

T_{DVN} = Torque of Driven Gear

T_{DVR} = Torque of Driver Gear

PCD_{DVN} = Pitch Circle Diameter of Driven Gear

PCD_{DVR} = Pitch Circle Diameter of Driver Gear

PCD_{ci} = Pitch Circle Diameter of Compound Input Gear

PCD_{co} = Pitch Circle Diameter of Compound Output Gear

Calculate Torque Using Number of Teeth

This ratio can also be calculated using the number of teeth.

Compound Gear Drive Torque Using Number of Teeth

$$\frac{T_{DVN}}{T_{DVR}} = \frac{N_{DVN}}{N_{DVR}} \times \frac{N_{ci}}{N_{co}}$$

Where:

T_{DVN} = Torque of Driven Gear

T_{DVR} = Torque of Driver Gear

N_{DVN} = Number of Teeth on Driven Gear

N_{DVR} = Number of Teeth on Driver Gear

N_{ci} = Number of Teeth on Compound Input Gear

N_{co} = Number of Teeth on Compound Output Gear

Segment 2 Multiple Shaft Drive Installation

Objective 4   Describe How to Determine the Direction of Rotation of a Gear Drive

Description of Direction of Rotation

Each gear that is added to a gear train causes the driven gear's rotation direction to change.

When there are only two gears, the driven gear turns in the opposite direction to the driver gear.

If one gear is added in the middle, either an idler gear or another driven gear, the direction of rotation of the original driven gear will be the same as the driver gear.

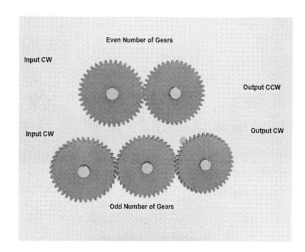

Description of the Even/Odd Rule

To determine the direction of rotation of a gear drive, you can remember that an even number of gears in the drive causes the driven gear to turn in the opposite direction and an odd number of gears causes the driven gear to turn in the same direction as the driver gear.

The exception to the even/odd rule is for compound gear drives.

In this case, you should treat gears that are on the same shaft as one gear.

Even/Odd Rule Example

For example, the compound gear drive shown here has four gears.

Since two gears are on the same shaft, the number of gears to use with the even/odd rule is three.

Therefore, the driven gear turns in the same direction as the driver gear. In this case, it is clockwise.

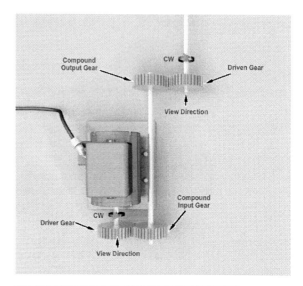

Effect of Perspective

A final point to remember about the direction of rotation is that these rules are based on looking at the rotation of the output shaft from the same side from which you viewed the input shaft.

If you are viewing the output shaft from the opposite side, the direction of rotation is reversed.

For example, the output shaft turns clockwise when you look at the shaft from the side indicated by the arrow.

From the opposite side, the shaft turns counterclockwise.

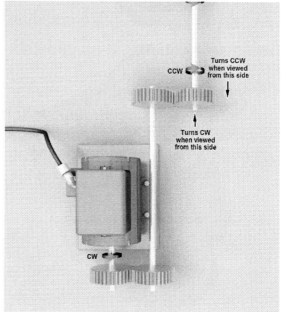

Objective 5 Describe How to Install and Align a Multiple Shaft Drive System

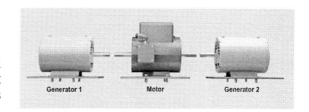

Order of Alignment

Each shaft in a multiple shaft drive system must be individually aligned. The alignment procedures for each shaft are the same as those for a single shaft drive system.

Although each shaft in the system must be individually aligned, there is a certain order in which to align the shafts.

Normally, the order of alignment is to start with the last output shaft in the drive and work backwards toward the driver shaft.

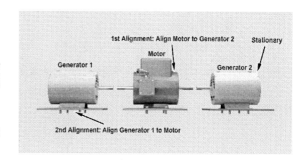

Order of Alignment Example

For example, Generator 2 and the Motor should be aligned first and Generator 1 and the Motor last.

For the first alignment, the Motor is the moveable machine.

For the second alignment, the Motor is the stationary machine while Generator 1 acts as the moveable machine.

Before Alignment

Before you start the installation and alignment procedure, determine the actual height of each shaft.

To allow shims to be added to the shaft during the alignment procedure, the driven shaft of each component should be slightly higher than the driver shaft.

The amount of difference in height depends on how uneven the surface is.

A good height difference to start with is 0.010 to 0.015 inch.

Each shaft must be progressively lower than the one downstream.

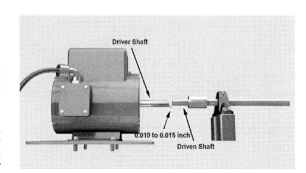

In-Line Shaft Alignment

For in-line shafts, the centerlines of the two shafts must be in line with each other.

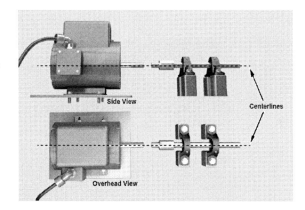

Adjacent Shaft Alignment

For adjacent shaft power transmission, the centerlines of the two shafts only have to be parallel with each other.

The shaft heights can be different to a certain degree without affecting the operation.

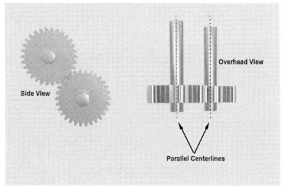

Segment 3   Sleeve Couplings

Objective 6   Describe the Function of a Solid Coupling and List Two Types

Solid Coupling Description

Solid couplings connect two shafts together to make them a rigid unit.

They are used when it is necessary to either extend the length of a shaft or provide a means of disconnecting the shaft.

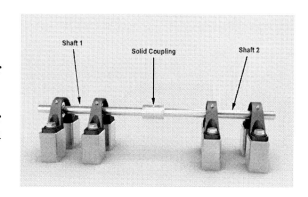

Solid Coupling Application

Solid couplings are rarely used to connect motors to driven components such as pumps and gearboxes because they do not allow any misalignment.

The only exception is when there is the need for absolute alignment.

The two most common types of solid couplings are sleeve couplings and flange couplings.

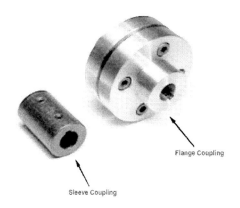

Objective 7   Describe the Operation of a Sleeve Coupling and Give an Application

Solid Sleeve Coupling Description

Sleeve couplings can be either solid or split.

The solid sleeve coupling is a solid cylinder of metal which is designed to slide over the two shafts and clamp them together by means of a set screw on each shaft.

To install this type, the two shafts must be able to be moved away from each other.

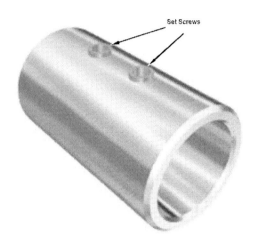

Solid Sleeve Coupling

Split Sleeve Coupling Description

The split sleeve coupling clamps the two shafts together using two half-round pieces that clamp to each other using bolts.

The split feature allows the two coupling halves to be removed without moving the two shafts away from each other.

The split sleeve coupling usually has ribs on its outer casing.

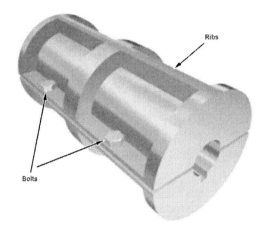

Split Sleeve Coupling

Sleeve Coupling Application

Sleeve couplings are mainly used on smaller shafts having diameters less than six inches, while larger shafts use flange couplings.

Since they do not allow any misalignment, they are mainly used on longer shafts.

This is because any misalignment in longer shafts can be compensated by the distance between the bearings.

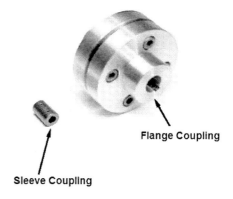

Flange Coupling

Sleeve Coupling

Objective 8   Describe the Alignment Procedure of a Sleeve Coupling

Sleeve Coupling Installation

The basic procedure for installing and aligning a sleeve coupling begins with leveling the two shafts and making them the same height.

Before doing this, place the sleeve coupling on one of the two shafts to be coupled and slide it back on the shaft. Then level and align the shafts.

The process is completed by sliding the coupling onto the other shaft and clamping it to each shaft.

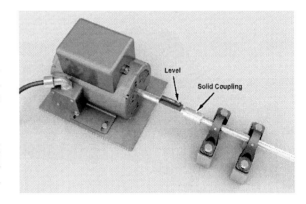

Sleeve Coupling Application

In some cases, the sleeve coupling is used to extend the length of a shaft by connecting another shaft that is not independently supported.

Here, there is not any alignment to be done.

Simply insert the extension shaft through the bearing on its end; slide the sleeve onto the other end of the shaft; and bring the two shafts together so that each shaft is inserted into the coupling and the gap between the two shafts is approximately 0.125 inch.

Floating Shaft Application

Another application of this concept is a floating shaft that is not supported directly by any bearings.

This shaft connects two other shafts using two solid couplings.

After aligning the supported shafts, the floating shaft can be installed without any further alignment necessary.

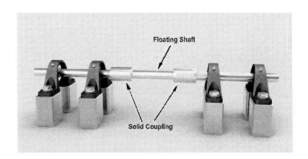

Glossary

Accuracy: A measure of how closely an instrument's output matches the actual value of the process variable.

Alignment: Being in the proper position; arranged in a linear fashion.

Aluminum: Element 13 on the periodic table, aluminum is a soft, light metal that resists corrosion.

Automatic: Having the ability of starting, operating, or moving independently.

Automatically: Moving or starting by itself.

Beam: A long, rigid, horizontal component used for structural support.

Bearing: A bearing is a device used to support another part while reducing friction at the point of contact.

Brake caliper: A housing that contains one or more pistons which press brake pads against a brake disc when hydraulic power is applied.

Brake disc: The brake disc is attached to the rotating device to be slowed. Friction is created when the brake caliper presses the brake pads against the disc, slowing the device.

Cantilever: A structural component that sticks out, or protrudes, from a rigid support.

Caustics: Substances capable of burning, corroding or destroying by chemical action. Acids and bases are common caustics.

Centerline: Centerlines are used to show an object's symmetry, or the center location of a rounded feature such as a hole. They are drawn using alternating dashes, one long dash followed by one short dash.

Clutch: A device that connects two shafts together and allows the shafts to connect and disconnect while running.

Coil: (Electricity) A coil is a winding of a conductor into a series of loops. This winding causes the electromagnetic fields around the coil to increase and it tends to resist any changes in current flow.
(PLCs) A coil is a ladder diagram symbol that represents an output instruction.
(Thermal Systems) A heat exchanger used to transfer energy from one source to another.

Component: A part of a larger, interacting system.

Compression: A process of applying pressure to a vapor, compacting the molecules closer together.

Compressor: (Thermal Systems) The central component of a heat pump system. The

---

compressor increases the pressure of a refrigerant vapor, and simultaneously reduces its volume, while causing the vapor to move through the system.
(Fluid Power) In a pneumatic system, the compressor takes the air from the atmosphere and compresses it. The compressed air is stored in a tank until it is needed by an application.

Computer numerical control: Computer numerical control is a manufacturing process that uses a computer to control the cutting tool motion.

Configuration: (General) The geometry of a part; its density, weight, and other visual parameters that uniquely characterize the item, component, or assembly.
(Information Technology) The way a computer or program is put together for a particular use.

Controller: (Control Systems) A controller is a hardware device or a software program that manages or directs the flow of data between two entities.
(Information Technology) In computing, controllers may be cards, microchips or separate hardware devices for the control of a peripheral device.
(General) In a general sense, a controller can be thought of as something or someone that interfaces between two systems and manages communications between them.

Coordinates: A set of two or more numbers used to determine the position of a point, line, curve, or plane.

Corrosion: Damage to a material (e.g. metal, skin, fabric) through a chemical process.

Corrosive: Capable of eating away; erosive; steadily harmful; gradually destructive. Corrosives are also called caustics.

Coupling: (Manufacturing) A coupling is the connector found on the end of a hose that allows the hose to be connected to a tool.
(Mechanics) A component used to connect two shafts, used when it is necessary to extend a shaft or provide a means for disconnecting a shaft.

Current: The movement of electrically charged particles through solids, liquids, gases, or free space. Electrical current is a measure of the amount of electrical charge transferred per unit time. It represents the flow of electrons through a conductive material.

Cycle: (Electricity) The time period required for a sinusoid to complete one cycle is called a full cycle. The time period when the sinusoid is positive is called the positive half cycle, and the time period when the sinusoid is negative is called the negative half cycle.
(Machining) The time it takes for a machine to complete its operation.

Cycloidal: The curve traced by a point on the circumference of a circle that rolls on a straight line.

Cylinder: A device that converts fluid power into linear mechanical power.

Density: Density is the amount of mass something has for a given volume, and is expressed in units of pounds per cubic foot (lb/ft^3) or kilograms per cubic meter (kg/m^3). For example, 1 m^3 of water has a mass of 1,000 kg, so the density of water is 1,000 kg/m^3.

Diameter: The diameter is the longest straight line or measurement within a circle that is terminated by the circle's periphery. This circle may be a planar section of a sphere or cylinder.

Differential: (Thermal Systems) The difference in the cut-in and cut-out temperatures, which is defined by a thermostat setting.
(General) Of, or relating to, a difference.

Dimension: A dimension is a measurement in length, width, thickness, or in a given direction

Diol: A chemical compound containing two hydroxyl groups.

Efficiency: The ratio of output to input that is usually expressed as a percentage.

Electrical: Of, relating to, producing, or operated by electricity.

Electromagnetic: Subject matter related to the interaction of electricity and magnetic fields.

Electron: A negatively charged component of an atom.

Environment: The conditions surrounding a component, including such things as dust, high/low humidity, water, grease, high/low temperature, high/low air flow.

Equipment: The tools, machines, or other things that are needed for a particular job or activity.

FHP: Fractional Horsepower - A fractional horsepower (FHP) motor has a rated output of less than one horsepower.

Flange: A projecting flat rim, collar, or rib on an object, for strength, for guiding, or for attachment to another object.

Fluid: The conducting material in a fluid power system, either a liquid (in hydraulic systems) or a gas (in pneumatic systems).

Force: (Mechanics) An influence exerted on an object. It can cause the object to move.
(General) Strength or energy as an attribute of physical action or movement.

Friction: The resistance to motion due to contact between two surfaces.

Geometry: Geometry is a math discipline that deals with the relationships of points, lines, angles, and figures.

Head: The height of a column of fluid that can be supported by the pressure supplied by a given pump, expressed in meters or feet.

Horizontal: Parallel to level ground.

Humidity: Humidity represents the amount of water vapor present in the atmosphere.
Hydraulic: A power transmission method that uses a pressurized liquid.

Indicator: An indicator is a device, such as a light, providing specific information on the state or condition of something.

Input: The current or voltage applied to an electric or electronic circuit or device.

Insert: An indexable insert is an insert that has multiple cutting edges. When the edge being used becomes worn or damaged, the insert is removed and indexed to expose a new cutting edge.

Intermittent: (General) Something that starts and stops irregularly
(Electricity) An intermittent energy source is any energy source that is not continuously available.

Involute: A curve traced by the end of a string wound upon another curve, or unwound from it.

Jack: (Mechanics) A device for exerting pressure or lifting a heavy body a short distance.
(Electricity) A female fitting in an electrical circuit designed for the insertion of a plug.

Junction: A transition layer or boundary between two different materials or between physically different regions in a single material, especially.

Load: (Electricity) Power output or power consumption.
(Mechanics) The external resistance overcome by an engine or machine.
(General) The quantity that can be carried at one time by a specific means.

Lubricant: A substance that is used to reduce friction between moving components.

MTBM: Machine to be Moved

Machining: Process of making, preparing, or finishing with a machine or with machine tools.

Manufacturer: A manufacturer is a person or group that makes goods or wares.

Measurement: The dimension, quantity, or capacity determined by measuring

Mechanical: Caused by, resulting from, or relating to a process that involves a purely physical process.

Misalignment: Not in the proper position; arranged in a non-linear fashion.

Neoprene: A synthetic polymer resembling rubber, resistant to oil, heat, and weathering.

Offset: An imaginary coordinate system based on a shift of position from the CNC machine's home position.

Operator: A person who operates a machine.

Output: The current, voltage, power, or signal produced by an electrical or electronic circuit or device.
Parallel: Lines, planes, surfaces, or objects having the same distance continuously

between them.

Parameter: A number or other measurable value that defines a system or sets the conditions of machine operation.

Period: The amount of time it takes for a repeating waveform to complete one cycle of all of its values.

Perpendicular: having the trait of meeting a line or surface at right angles.

Pitch: (Mechanics) On a bolt, the pitch is the distance from the crest of one individual thread to the crest of the next individual thread.
(Green Energy Technology) In wind turbines, pitch refers to the angle of a rotor blade with respect to the plane of the rotor.

Pneumatic: A power transmission method that uses compressed gas, typically air.

Polyester: Polymers formed from dicarboxylic acid and a diol.

Polymer: A large molecule that is made up of many repeating base units. Natural examples include hair fibers and DNA. Modern plastic materials are synthetic polymers.

Pressure: The intensity of force created when a force from one object acts over the area of another. Pressure can be calculated by the formula: pressure = force / area.

Program: A sequence of instructions, written to perform a specified task with a computer or controller.

Programmable logic controller: A programmable logic controller (also called a "PLC" or simply a "programmable controller") is a computer used for automation of electromechanical processes, such as control of machinery on factory assembly lines and in process control. Unlike general-purpose computers, the PLC is designed to be used in an industrial environment and typically includes multiple inputs and output arrangements, extended temperature ranges, immunity to electrical noise, and resistance to vibration and impact.

Refrigerant: A fluid of extremely low boiling point used to transfer heat between the heat source and heat sink. It absorbs heat at low temperature and low pressure and rejects heat at a higher temperature and higher pressure, usually involving changes of state in the fluid.

Resistance: A property of a conductor where it opposes or resists the movement of current in the conductor. Equal to the voltage across the conductor divided by the current flowing in the conductor. Usually measured in ohms.

Signal: An electrical quantity, such as current or voltage, that can be varied in a way to convey information.

Software: Software is a general term for the various kinds of programs used to operate computers and related devices. It may also be referred to as a software application.

Spindle: The main component of the machine tool that rotates. In milling, the spindle holds a cutting tool. On a lathe the spindle holds the workpiece.

Standard: A thing established for comparison by an authority or by a consensus agreement.

Straightness: Straightness is a feature of size that specifies the amount a feature can vary from a straight line.

Symmetry: Symmetry is the trait of being made up of like parts equally placed from a common feature.

Synchronous: Existing or occurring at the same time.

Synthetic: Materials or substances produced from chemicals by way of human manipulation.

Tag: Text-based names given to PLC memory locations used to store information to the PLC about both internal and external conditions.

Tap: (Machining) A tool used to create threads in a hole.
(Fluid Power) A device that controls the flow of a liquid or a gas through a pipe or other container.
(Electricity) A tap is a connection on the secondary coil that creates the ability to obtain multiple levels of voltage from the secondary coil of a transformer.

Technician: A worker in a field of technology who is trained in the applicable skills and techniques, with a relatively practical understanding of the theoretical principles.

Thermal: Relating to or caused by heat.

Tolerance: The allowable deviation from nominal that is still considered acceptable.

Torque: A force that makes an object rotate about a point.

Transformer: An electrical device that converts AC electricity from one voltage level to another.

Transmission: (Mechanics) A system that converts force, often from a high-speed, low-torque motor to a lower-speed, higher-torque output device.
(Electricity) The process of sending electricity or data using electrical signals or electromagnetic waves from one place to another.

UNC: Unified National Coarse. UNC is a general-purpose thread type commonly used in assembly work. It has fewer threads per inch than other thread types.

Vertical: Perpendicular to level ground.

Voltage: A measure of the difference in electric potential between two points in space, a material, or an electric circuit, expressed in volts, and represented with the variable V. Also referred to as electromotive force (EMF) and represented with the variable E.

Workpiece: A part that is being worked on. It may be subject to cutting, welding, forming, or other operations.